Citizens of Nowhere

Citizens of Nowhere

an anthology

Edited by Debz Hobbs-Wyatt and Gill James

Bridge House

British Library Cataloguing in Publication Data

A Record of this Publication is available from the British
Library

ISBN 978-1-907335-53-2

This edition published 2017 by Bridge House Publishing
Manchester, England

All Bridge House books are published on paper derived
from sustainable resources.

Contents

Introduction

Theresa May sparked a powerful debate when she announced that global citizens were citizens of nowhere. She also gave us a marvellous title and a great theme for a book.

Many, myself included, found May's statement disturbing. I'm British. There is much about being British and the British that I love but not quite everything and not at the cost of appreciating aspects of other cultures. I can't help it. I've lived abroad. I've taught modern languages for twenty-six years and in doing so used international friendship and communication as a motivator. I'm married to the son of a World War II / Holocaust refugee. He brings a lot of German qualities and a few Jewish ones to our everyday lives. Many of my teen years were spent with Elaine, Ingrid, Monica, Theo and Rene – all born in Jamaica and I never noticed the colour of their skin. Eating sweet-potatoes at a 4.00 p.m. dinner felt normal. Elaine and Ingrid's mum was a great cook and kept to her Jamaican domestic clock.

These are mainly commissioned pieces. A handful were submitted to other anthologies but seemed incredibly appropriate for this one.

Our collection begins with Alan Gibbons' *From Our Own Correspondent*. What would we look like to visiting aliens? Alan responded to my request for a story by saying that maybe he could do this. Within an hour he'd come up with an idea and another hour later the text was on my computer.

Jenny Palmer's story completes the collection. I loved this story so much that this will be the fourth time I publish it. It first appeared on the CaféLit site, then in *The Best of CaféLit 6* and is also in her single author collection. You'll understand why when you read the last line.

We have a delightful mixture of interpretations of the citizen of nowhere.

In *Slowly Things Appear* Ea Anderson brings us a story of alienation, the global citizen always on the move away from something, through and towards the unknown.

By contrast, Neil Campbell's *These Boots Were made for Walking* is firmly set in a Manchester that many of us know so well. It is a multi-cultural Manchester that worries about Brexit. My own story *The Wedding Next Door* shows how cultures can rub along together though it's not always easy. Matevž Hönn juxtaposes for us in *Perfect Day* events across the globe which seem curiously connected. Debz Hobbs-Wyatt's *Boarding House* is indeed about a boarding house but one where all sorts of people from all sorts of situations have to get along and in doing this they get to know themselves better.

Vanessa Gebbie kindly gifted us a recycled story: her *The Kettle on the Boat.* This is beautifully told in a child's voice. The story gives us a great insight into another culture. The child moves into another as yet to her unknown culture. We feel her fear. No, being a global citizen is not easy.

Karen Kendrick's *The Road to Nowhere* presents a modern day problem: political refugees. Her story shows both sides of this problem in very human terms. A similar theme is explored in Vanessa Harbour's *Home,* but this time we have a child's point of view.

Shqiperia by Jennifer Burkinshaw shows us two people struggling with two cultures. Sarah Dobbs tackles another form of Otherness in her story *Something like Mohammed.* Discrimination isn't just about race. Neither is diversity.

7

Global citizens face many difficulties and in many cases in the stories here they grow because they overcome huge obstacles. Should we not therefore welcome them and perhaps rename them citizens of everywhere?

Gill James

From our own correspondent

Alan Gibbons

Stardate: xiL009877
(Earth time: June 16, 2016)

This is Orwys Interfarian on planet Earth, a small green and blue spherical, life-sustaining planet some six trillion Vetroceps from home. All across the universe, these colours, blue for the delicious combination of hydrogen and oxygen known as water, white for its fluffy, airborne manifestation known as cloud and green for vegetation, symbolise life in all its sublime, fecund, teeming variety. Imagine my excitement as I prepare to set foot on this lush, mineral-rich haven spinning in a far distant void, certain that here, beyond numerous asteroid belts, dying stars and endless, echoing emptiness, here I would find hospitality, generosity and species solidarity.

Is the camera rolling, guys? OK, cool, let's take our first step on the surface of this verdant, gentle world. There is a settlement up ahead, known on planet Earth as a city. Ah, here we have a large monument. It is a giant image erected on poles. Clearly, the Earthlings are proud of this, my first example of terrestrial artwork. I will interview this passing humanoid. Just give me a few moments while I put my questions. Well, that was... unsettling. It transpires that some four or five million Earthlings are on the move, desperate to avoid want, violence and war. It seems that this species extracts base metals and fossil fuels in huge quantities in order to shred each other's bodies in constant conflict. Still, that said, I am warmed by the sentiments expressed on this artwork.

Breaking point.

There we have it. Faced with suffering humanity, this orange man here, Nipple Porridge I think his name is, is making a strong statement. There is a moral breaking point, beyond which no Earthling would go. Look at these poor people, he is telling us. Look at their courage, their endurance, their.... Excuse me, the humanoid I was interviewing is trying to say something. What's that? Sorry, I don't understand. Let's cut the transmission for a moment.

Right, we're back. He is saying that the displaced people – or migrants – are *not* welcome. Nipple Porridge wants them to go back. I am not quite sure what he means by *back*. After all, haven't they just come from somewhere intolerable? Why would they return to somewhere like that? Now, hold on, let's re-run that last section so I can get this quite clear. Porridge wants them to return to an endless landscape of shattered buildings and roving, murderous armed men? What sense does that make? Sorry? Yes. Yes. Thank you. So Porridge thinks these helpless people, with their few belongings are going to harm their hosts? Have I got that right?

I think we will pause our broadcast there. This is rather bewildering. Without further information, I don't feel equipped to editorialise. I will address this issue further in my next report.

This is Orwys Interfarian on Planet Earth.

Goodnight.

Stardate: xiL009881
(Earth time: August, 2016)

This is Orwys Interfarian on planet Earth, investigating another aspect of the movement of poor, frightened people across the globe. I am now in a corner of north-eastern France, a fragment of a land mass called Europe. I have been absent from your screens for a little while as I researched the concept of *country*. The Earthlings seem to arbitrarily divide land masses into states or countries. Sometimes they find a relatively plausible reason to do this, a range of raised ground called a mountain, a ribbon of water called a river or some other geographical feature. On other occasions, they simply draw an imaginary line across a patch of ground. This in spite of the fact that the beings to either side of the line share identical DNA. Even more confusing, they lay claim to areas of water. Even though they are unable to stand on water or erect homes on it, they say it belongs to their country, even though it tends to travel back and forth in movements called waves.

Anyway, I think I can safely say that, though there is little rhyme or reason to the arbitrary setting of these lines, or borders, between the various states or countries, humans become very agitated about their invisible lines. It is for this reason that some humans board small, leaking waterborne vehicles to reach safety while other humans board larger, sometimes armed, waterborne vehicles to stop them reaching safety. This practice is called national security, which oddly, though related, appears to be the opposite of safety. I have been both surprised and appalled to discover that, rather than share out the people escaping death and poverty among them, the inhabitants of the richer countries, seem unconcerned that five thousand of the poor, frightened *migrants* are now lying dead at the bottom of the sea. Apparently, all life on Earth is sacred, but some lives are more sacred than others.

I asked a representative of one of the more fortunate, richer, arbitrarily-decided land masses to explain this

11

practice of permitting people to perish or, if they survive, subsist in sub-standard accommodation called *camps* or even *jungles* (oddly, there are few trees in these jungles, which are different to the jungles that have trees and animals). He introduced me to a number of new concepts. One was *swamping*. This is the practice of permitting relatively modest numbers of poor people to live among rich people. Another is *culture*. These are the arbitrary practices conducted by some of the people in the arbitrarily established bits of land called countries. He also said that he wanted his country back even though I couldn't find any evidence whatsoever that it had ever been anywhere else. Finally, he seemed keen to find a special prize called a red, white and blue Brexit which appears to be a kind of biscuit which you eat for breakfast on special occasions called referenda.

My enquiries took me to the jungle you will see before you called The Jungle. What made this jungle more jungle-ish than any of the smaller jungles I could not understand. In this treeless collection of primitive shacks live hundreds of poor people who would like to live with rich people across a ribbon of water called the Channel though the humans here in France called it the Munch or sleeve. I think this may be because Earthlings eat their sleeves then drink a portion of the sea to wash it down. From time to time, black-clad men and women called police shoot pieces of metal and canisters of stinging gas at the poor people to welcome them to their country. This makes the poor people angry, which leads them to climb fences and jump on vehicles called trucks. Some of the poor people fall under the trucks. Oddly, this does not lead the leaders of the rich people to change how they run their countries. Instead, they build bigger fences. I suggested erasing the arbitrary lines called borders to facilitate the movement of people where they want to go. They said I was a dreamer. I said surely I wasn't the only one.

Stardate: xiL009887
(Earth time: December, 2016)

I have just returned from a land mass called Syria. It is from here that many people have fled across many land masses to avoid being killed. I have prepared a simple explanation of what has been happening so that you will understand why the people from Syria do not stay in Syria. Some of the people from Syria did not like the way the government (small groups of people who run the affairs of larger groups of people) governed so they protested. The government hurt their children so they protested more loudly. The government then killed those who were protesting loudly. Soon, the government was killing the people they governed and inviting people from other countries to help them kill the people they governed. Two of the biggest countries in the world had something called *interes*ts in this country far away and did not like each other so they called on different groups of poor people and encouraged medium-sized countries to help. The leader of one of these countries is rich, but does not have a shirt and travels on an animal called a horse rather than a vehicle propelled by fossil fuel. The new leader of the other big country wears the hair of another life form and likes building walls as a hobby. Other groups of people had faith in peace so they also killed people so there would be more peace, which seemed contradictory, but appeared to make sense to those involved. Anyway, that is the simple version of the story they told me and that is why the country called Syria, which used to have houses now has piles of rubble and lots of dead bodies.

On my way back, I went to see what was happening to the Jungle. When I arrived I found that the Jungle was now a patch of ground with no primitive shacks at all which the government there thought was better than a patch of ground with primitive shacks. One night the police came and took away the people and knocked down the shacks. They then moved the poor people who wanted to cross the Channel further away from the Channel. This would help preserve interests and security by not securing things in the interests of anybody, at least that is what the chief of police told me.

I am close to the end of my journey and I think I have at last made some sense of what I have seen. Most people on this planet want to live in peace and have enough to eat and drink. They want to sit in small dwellings and look at rectangular screens that glow. They laugh and stick smaller glowing screens to their heads and press small buttons and like things. They pass around pictures with untrue statements called memes. This makes them laugh and nod their heads. They do not want other people to hit, shoot or burn them or make them cross land masses or fall into salty water, but sometimes some of them get shot and burned and cross land masses and fall into salty water even though there seems to be enough food, water, land masses, dwellings and glowing screens for everybody.

The problem seems to be a word called *profit*. This means some people own the guns and aeroplanes and houses and food and water and screens and make money from them. Money is sometimes made of paper, plastic or metal and sometimes it is a digit on one of the glowing screens. It makes people who have it happy and people who do not have it unhappy. *Profit* by the way is different to *prophet* which is somebody who tells you something which may or may not be true, depending on your opinion. Because of profit, the extra money some people extract, not prophet, the person who tells you things, some people have more homes and food and water and screens and bombs and guns than other people and sometimes there are fights over who has things and who doesn't. When there are these fights, some people leave their homes and end up with nothing at all then the people who have things say they will be swamped by people who don't so they drown them or leave them in jungles. The wanting of more homes, food, water, screens, bombs and guns seems to be addictive. The more the rich people have the more they seem to want. In this process they seem to lose any feeling or sympathy for the people who have nothing.

After my six months on planet Earth, I would like to conclude my report by saying that I understand all this and have been able to suggest some solutions to its problems. Sadly, I do not and have not, but there is hope because I have seen a man on a glowing screen who does seem to have a solution. The man is called Siren Growl and may be non-terrestrial as he has an unusual square head. He says that the solution is something called the X-Factor, a quasi-magical force that makes people scream and talk into their small glowing screens while watching their large glowing screens. While they are experiencing the X-Factor, they forget the poor people that are moving around the world and feel happy.

Before I return home, I hope to get my hands on some X-Factor and discover its properties.

This is Orwys Interfarian on planet Earth.

Goodnight and may peace be with you.

15

Slowly Things Appear

Ea Anderson

I have been thinking about an escape. It's not an escape through woods. It's not either an escape through a city or in a shoreline on a beach. I'm not even running. I think. I don't think I'm running. Maybe I will walk down the stairs at night with a suitcase in my hand. Maybe I will walk down the stairs in full daylight. I might have tickets in my pocket and I might touch them. Keep my hand on them, protective, reassuring. I might just have an idea. I might have called somebody in the morning or the night before, while my eyes were fixed on a cloud outside, while my eyes wouldn't leave this cloud. Or a tree. I might have given hints, names of cities out of context, countries, field or town, seaside or somewhere deep in the centre of a continent.

I will cry. Hard and long. Unstoppable. Sob in toilets, next to my suitcase. Then stop. Then start. Then pull myself together, then rip myself apart. I think that it will come to an end, but it might not. I let it come. I don't control it.

I will stay in a flat, bare, only furnished with necessities. I only pull myself together to go out to get food, or a meal, or a cup of coffee at a café and it's soothing.

I might wear big dark sunglasses and fall into old habits. I will pull myself into rhythm. But first make a rhythm. Breakfast, lunch, dinner, sleep. Don't get up if you wake at night. Don't get up before six and no later than nine. Then, after months, things might be filled into this rhythm. When it's safe. I might stay up later or go to bed really early, something like seven o'clock. Go to a museum and just leave again without having seen anything, indecisive.

16

No! I can't speak of these things, they are too alien, these extra things. Not even picturable. Don't make a new life I tell myself. Be simple. Be a rhythm. Fulfil basic needs, but hardly do that.

There might be a nice park across the street where I will go. Where I will lie in the sun on my back in the grass. I refuse to recognise it's the sun and then I don't. I just feel the warmth. It is just warmth. Very warm on me. That's all. Don't think about where it comes from. And then it disappears.

By now the crying has stopped. I long for it. Deep down I'm longing for it. This deep down is not that deep since the longing is so big, too big.

I go to a church at night. At a side entrance in a building connected to the church, people are streaming in. I go into the church and try to sit on a church bench. I can't, I don't seem to be able to sit there for long. It's out of control. I go outside again. The people are still streaming in through the side entrance. Into a neutral room, coldly lit. There are old informative posters on the walls and on a table, leaflets about health and other things I know nothing of and have no interest in. It's a cold night, clear, with stars. The big trees are dark, they rattle as I leave, as I walk down the street, away.

Might this become a pattern, a part of the rhythm? One of the things I fill in? A safe thing, not alien, though I understand nothing. I go there most nights. Often, mostly, the people are there. But once in a while they are not. It might be a holiday that has slipped me by like most holidays. Then the streets are either empty and the door closed, or the church is full and hymns and organ music fill the street. I listen to it from the outside or standing in the church's enormous doorway.

But most nights they are there. I don't go in, I stay

outside and mix with them in their break. Without speaking, they nod at me.

I have started regularly visiting the Chinese grocery store. The woman is so short and square. She keeps nodding at me, almost bowing, saying sounds that are not meant to be words. I buy lemonade I retrieve from the fridge, and tea. I buy vegetables whose names I don't know and have no idea how to prepare. I put them on a plate in the kitchen. I leave them there. I glance at them when I pass them. Sometimes I go to the kitchen just with the purpose of looking at them. I buy noodles and put them into boiling water for a minute, and eat them just like that, with a fork, straight out of the boiling water. It is comforting to eat food with so little nutrition, so bland, so raw in a way. The noodles are the colour of a sick person's skin.

Might somebody call me some day? How, where did they get my number? I look at the ringing phone. I freeze, not in fear there is no room for that. In wonder. I agree it must be somebody selling something, shares of flats in Florida or righteous feelings through charity. I have no charity left in me. I pull a chair over to the phone and keep looking at it.

Now there's a park across the street with warmth, a church, people streaming through a side entrance, meal, a café, the Chinese grocery store, the woman in the Chinese grocery store, lemonade, tea, strange vegetables, noodles, and a phone that rings. I wonder what all these things are, together.

And my suitcase lying open on the floor just inside the living room door, still not unpacked, the clothes messed around in it. There's also the warm day and the cold nights with stars. There's a side street I pass, warm light shines from steamy windows. It's restaurants, cafes, a shop with

18

precious old things. I have not walked down this street. I stop at the end of it, the entrance. I can see all the way to the other end, it's a straight street. I haven't walked down this street yet. I watch it. I look down it. I guess I like to watch things, to see them from the outside.

It looks so real, so much like life. I walk on then and go to the Pakistani grocery store that's open all night. There're strip lights in the ceiling and long rows of candy you can choose and put in a little bag with a little shovel. I do that. I take my time, I can't decide. I leave the bags of candy on the kitchen table. I don't eat it. Sometimes, sometimes I open a bag of candy and look inside, sugar like diamonds or ice crystals, many colours, pink, acid green, see-through red and blue. I feel like a prisoner. Somebody who's been let out and just can't shake it.

I must allow myself something. To unpack, to fold my clothes, to drink coffee in the morning. The sweets. To eat something sweet, slowly. No! Just the thought confuses me, my words stumble and end up in piles in my head, in my mouth entangled. It reminds me of something like anger. I twitch. I just sit in the bathroom for a while then, on top of the toilet. It's white and has no windows the bathroom.

Then the phone rings again. Does it really? I stick my head out of the bathroom door and look at it, the phone in the living room. It's not moving, it's quiet. Then it rings again. I go over there, with firm steps I go to the phone.

"Hello," I say. My voice in this room with no other sounds. It surprises me. Who does it sound like? "Yes, hello now," I say, to confirm. It's a neighbour. I had never thought of that, that I have neighbours. I try to sound nice, welcoming. Something doesn't work. The neighbour is talking. It's about a meeting about problems with the garbage. Cats, rats, something roaming through, splitting open the black bags and spreading the content in the

19

courtyard. "Seagulls maybe," I suggest.

"No," the woman says. They want to put up a fence.

"Yes, I see," I say, "Oh." I have moved to the window. I have the phone in my hand. I look out the windows and then I see the buildings, the other buildings with maybe hundreds of lights turned on in other flats. I had not noticed them before. I look from side to side, do I maybe expect to see the woman from the other end of my phone standing in one of those windows? Then it occurs to me that she might live in the same building as me. I look at the floor.

"Good then," she says, "seven thirty."

I'm exhausted when we hang up. Seven thirty, it's too late or too early.

And now it's night. I turn on a radio, some man is taking calls, then there's some music, then he takes calls again and it gets later and later. I sit in my bed under the covers. I look out the windows through the half closed blinds. One after another, the lights in the buildings turn off. But not all of them. I haven't gone to bed in that sense, I have just fallen asleep. I wake up and the radio is still on. I leave it on. It keeps surprising me, these sounds. They are from another world. I even smile at them. And then I notice I smile.

There are simply too many things now. I try to think of them one at the time. Food, streets, days, seasons. I then subdivide them. Noodles, vegetables, lemonade and tea under food. The street with the church and the side street under streets. Day and night, but then I'm not sure what they fit under. There are simply too many things and some of them don't fit into a category, they can't be fitted.

I go into a shop I have passed many times. It is nothing I have planned. I buy a lotion. I'm surprised when I stand on the street again, with the lotion in a bag in my hand. I take it out of the bag there on the street and look at it. For very dry skin, 24 hour moisturizing, pomegranate and peach. All fruity I think. In the flat, I put the lotion on a shelf in the bathroom. I apply it that night, to my legs and my arms. These touches feel strange. I spread the lotion on my legs, I rub it in. My legs seem very sensitive. I feel everything. The touches spread up through my body as something like electricity. It's not pleasant and it is not unpleasant. It is just new. I just notice it and note it. I add it to the list and remember.

For some reason it makes me feel like I should say something clear, try to make clear statements. Something firm. Just say something, full stop. Just for the sake it, saying something firm. I straighten up and look into the mirror but that's too much. I turn around. "It's Tuesday," I say. Then, "It's on Tuesday." I emphasise Tuesday. Then again, emphasizing on. It had some effect, but it didn't have enough of an effect, not as I expected. Maybe it does matter what you state firmly. I finish the lotion on my arms.

I walk along the building with the flat, two doors down I go in and walk up the staircase. On the third floor to the left, I ring the doorbell. A little tune starts behind the door. I hear voices, and steps closing in. I look down at myself, I must have got dressed, I wear black. A neutral skirt in a light fabric, a very soft tight woollen sweater. I keep stroking my arms to feel the softness. A big woman opens the door, she's so fat, I'm fascinated. Her fat keeps moving slowly in waves even though she's standing still. She lets me in.

"Margaret," she says and squeezes my hand. Her hand is warm and a little damp. I look at our hands touching. She's looking at me like she's waiting for something.

"Karen," I say then. I don't know where that came from.

My name is Karen. I chip in for the fence. From a handbag sitting next to my chair, I pull out twenty pounds and chip in. I carry the handbag home with me. It is black, a flap of brown calf skin with a magnet closes it. I examine it at the table in the flat. I like this bag. In a small compartment meant for small things is a little note. I unfold it, "Fence-day Saturday 10 PM," it says. I have written this note. My handwriting is careful and delicate. I put the note on the fridge with a magnet shaped like The Eiffel Tower.

Now this future day of fence lies as an impediment in my days. I keep remembering it, I remember it in the daytime, walking the streets letting things enter and leave me. And it stops me abrupt and hard. I remember it at night lying in this strange but familiar bed with white sheets, which I have started feeling some ownership over, looking at the warm square lights from the building across the street through the blinds. The memory enters me just as I'm dosing off, as my eyes are closing and everything around me feels like temperate tea with the structure of down. Then is comes hard and cold. I open my eyes, I'm not afraid, it's not that, it's a border through everything. I try to focus on my magic candy, my strange vegetables, my streets with untouchable mystery, but I can't get in touch with them.

Prosaic has entered. And won't leave.

I am thinking about an escape. It will be by train. It will take me through emerald green landscapes of rounded hills with sheep, and farmers waving from beside the tracks. It will take me through fields of vine, stony mountain ranges. I will look out the window and sometimes it will rain and streams of water will run down the window and other times the sun will shine. The suitcase sits next to me on the floor. The handbag lies on my lap. Other people will enter my carriage and sit across from me or next to me. We will nod. A man will offer me sections from his paper when he's done with them. I will accept with a smile but I won't read them. I let the newspapers lie in my lap with my hands resting on them. I keep looking out the window. Nobody else is going as far as I am, I will go on for days on this train and people keep entering and leaving. Sometimes the train stops for a long time at a bigger station in a city. I don't know for how long; I don't have a watch. I see the business of the bigger cities. Men in suits with briefcases, rushing, women with hats, women in red dresses waiting for men, tiny dogs with short legs moving fast, children on roller skates shouting to each other, newspaper salesmen, somebody playing guitar and singing for money, departures and arrivals announced over the speakers, a child gone missing, vending machines with cigarettes and coffee, an alarm going off, the smell of hot dogs and chestnuts, paper from sweeties spinning up and up in a draught and then the train will blow it's whistle and set in motion. I will get off at the end station. It's a small costal village and the track goes almost all the way into the sea. I ask at the ticket counter if they know of a place I can rent somewhere to stay. "Well," the old man says. He knows of a lady who might have something. I shake her hand as she leaves. Sand has been blown into the street. The cottage is at the end of the main street, to the left is the sea. Here I unpack. Here I step out of the door and stand on the street in an airy, impartial dress. The skirt lifts around my legs in the breeze. I turn my head and look to the sea. I turn my head and look towards the village. Salty drops in the air. Then I start walking.

These Boots Were Made for Walking

Neil Campbell

Lucy takes an old toothbrush and rubs the bristles of it between bathroom tiles. She buffs the taps in the sink so they gleam, and squirts bleach under the toilet rim before flushing. Then she climbs into the bath, and, on her hands and knees, scrubs at the white enamel.

Back in her bedroom, she clears the books and bits of paper off the floor and then hoovers the room. She hangs her onesie on the back of the door and then sprays the windows and wipes them clean. She goes downstairs and gets herself a cup of coffee before going back to her bedroom. She puts the coffee by the side of her bed and then gets into bed and reaches across for the laptop. Logging in to her email, she checks through the job alerts, saves a couple of application forms, and makes a start on one of them.

At lunch time she walks past Ali's barbers to Samir's, where she gets herself a bottle of Vimto, some avocados and a bag of oranges. Back in the kitchen, in the house she shares with Dave and Linda, she scoops out avocado and spreads it across toast. She goes back upstairs with her toast and an orange and puts the food at the side of the bed before going back downstairs for more coffee. Back in bed, she checks Twitter and Facebook while eating her lunch, and then resumes work on the novel she's writing, an Arts Council application form, and the transcribing of an interview with another woman with family from Guangzhou. It is part of the research for her next novel. Not the one she is writing now, the next one.

In the evening, she goes on a date with a man she's met

on Tinder. He talks about himself all evening, but at least he's confident and good looking. He buys her two drinks, which she doesn't have a problem with. He asks her where she's from, and when she says Manchester, he says "No, where are you from *originally*?" and when she says Manchester again he looks exasperated and asks, "Where do your *parents* come from then?" They agree to meet again, but she already knows she won't. She knows he doesn't like her, he likes her type. He has yellow fever.

As she is walking past Spinningfields towards her bus stop on Bridge Street, where she'll get the 38 back to Swinton, she hears something she has heard many times over the years. It is a drunk man, in a group of drunk men, and he says slyly to her, as she passes, "Love me long time ten dollar."

The effect on her is the same as always. She shouts back at him, much to his surprise, "Oh my God! Did you hear what your friend just said? That's so fucking racist!" But the man doesn't seem to hear her, or at least pretends not to, and neither he nor any of the other men look around. As they continue to walk away she stands there, the middle finger of each hand raised to the group. "Racists!" she shouts. "You're all racists!"

She grew up above the K P Wan in Droylsden. Her parents worked long hours, night after night, and the bulk of their business was done after the pubs closed. Before she started working there, Lucy was already aware of what the people were like who came in. She could hear their strange, garbled voices from upstairs, where she sat watching TV. She was never aware about having a choice about working there or not. Like for her younger brother, it seemed inevitable. In hindsight, she thinks her parents wanted to show her how it might be if she didn't study properly at college.

25

At first it wasn't so bad. She worked at tea time, and often it was old men or women, or an old couple, coming in for their regular weekly treat at the Chinese. They got Chow Mein, or fried rice, and they were polite. It was nice, they were friendly. They asked her what she wanted to be, if she was going to college, if she had a boyfriend. It was only when she got older and started working later that things became unpleasant. All those people that wandered in after drinking in The Moss Tavern, or The Cotton Tree, or The Snipe. They talked too loud and never looked her in the eye, instead pointing up at the menu and shouting a number. They leaned on the counter or against the wall and they smelled of beer, it was like gas from their breath as they spoke.

It was in the take away that she first heard someone say, "Love me long time, ten dollar." She didn't know what it meant, but she saw her father's face as he stopped briefly before carrying on wrapping paper around a tray. She wondered why the lads were laughing. She smiled at them, didn't know the joke, and that's what she felt sick about after she googled it.

The search engine came up with footage from the film, *Full Metal Jacket*. It was on YouTube and called 'The Hooker Scene'. With the song 'These Boots are Made for Walking' playing in the background, the camera follows a woman in a mini skirt and heels as she walks across the road to a couple of American soldiers sitting at a table. She propositions them, saying, "Me so horny, me love you long time." Lucy realizes that this is probably where it has come from. A Hollywood movie. It didn't seem to matter to those pissed people in the takeaway that the film was set in Vietnam, and that the hooker was Vietnamese. So, what did that make Lucy then, a hooker? How could she be a hooker, working in her parents' takeaway?

From then on, she wasn't so polite. She was ready for anything that someone might say, was waiting for it. One night a drunk man kept saying, over and over, that he wanted 'flied lice'. He said it so many times. He kept saying it while he and his friend waited. And every time he said it to his friend they both collapsed in drunken laughter. When his friend said that maybe he should stop, the first man said, "The Chinkies are used to it." *Chinkies.* That was another one. She looked at her mum who just smiled sadly. Her father had that same little look her gave her when the man said the ten dollar thing. But they both carried on working, putting food into trays, wrapping the trays in paper, putting them in carrier bags, placing them politely and carefully on the counter for the customers. When the man and his friend came to pick up their food from the counter, and he said, "flied lice" again, Lucy shouted, "FRIED RICE! FRIED RICE! FRIED RICE!" and the drunken lads looked surprised before laughing their heads off and leaving. They were still laughing as they walked past the window. A woman who had been waiting in the queue said, "I've changed my mind, there's no need for that," and asked for her money back.

Lucy didn't work there again. She thought it a natural reaction she'd had and didn't get it when her parents didn't back her up. But when she calmed down she realized it was for the business, and then she felt bad for them.

If anything, things seemed to be getting worse. The only good thing was that sometimes her east Asian background helped her to get her short stories published. She ticked that box. *About fucking time I got something out of it*, she thought. But society didn't seem to be improving. There was the whole Brexit thing, which came about because white people had had enough of immigration, and UKIP, with greasy Farage, and to top it all, Donald Trump, a sexist, racist man, getting elected president of the United States. It was Farage she hated the most. He was like the kind of man she saw all the time. The kind of man who would act like a dickhead in the takeaway and then smile at her if he saw her in town. It was a two-faced, sneaky kind of racism that made people think that things had improved, when they hadn't. The country was still ruled by the Oxbridge elite. Everyone on TV was still white. It was hard for Lucy to see how anything had changed. When Trump got elected for the U.S. presidency, she kicked a hole in the kitchen door.

She worked all day, and long into the evening, researching, applying for funding, polishing her novels and short stories. Her parents were still working in the takeaway. Business was booming. But racism clung to the walls of that building like grease. So, she didn't see her parents very often, and if she stopped to think about that she felt sad. But she couldn't afford to stop. She had work to do. She had to keep on working. She had to work for change. And when it wasn't going well, she hoovered the carpets, cleaned the windows, rubbed between bathroom tiles with an old toothbrush, put bleach in the toilet, buffed the taps, got in the bath on her hands and knees to scrub at the white enamel.

Something like Mohammed

Sarah Dobbs

Watching that young girl with the dark lad in my local, got me to thinking, it has. How I can remember when you were just a bundle of heat. Aye, proper smiler. Real, in my hands. I didn't have to grasp for your memory. Look at 'em, her white, him black. You wonder which side would even want them.

Me, I were never that good a kid. Some would say – Rita, if you asked, I suspect – that I were never a good man neither. In the 70s, we had this stray kitten decide we were it. New home. Refused to cuddle with me though. So I'd pin it till it stopped fighting. Proper devious little git. Soon as I let go, would you believe, it bolted faster than that Lightnin' Bolt, whatsisname. Same with women. Maybe that's why god hid my little lad, till I were ready, y'know? For love.

She's feeding the lad absolute junk. You've gotta think, what good's that gonna do him? He's clearly retarded. Enough to put you off your dinner. Never say that to their face, mind. Am no racist. And look at that hat. Indoors an all.

So that kitten grew up, cast right sly glances at me over its shoulder, like girls in the Magpie. I'd feel right thwarted. I tell everyone she left me (Rita). I go for long walks down the Leeds Liverpool and unravel the whole sorry story to fishermen. She cheated (also true). I was wronged (possibly not, though if I encourage my anger enough, I can believe it). Never love again, not after such betrayal.

Truth? Much easier to please yourself, intit. I walk into the village, get me Saturday fry-up. Half a pint before it's even acceptable. Read the paper myself. Don't have to pretend I don't notice Rita's sharpness at my ignorance of *world events*. Or to share the paper, heaven forbid. The way she'd just nestle in and we'd only get to turn the page when she were through. Such a slow reader – and she called me ignorant! I do sometimes go to the library to use the Facebook. I do sometimes type her school-friend's name in, the one who'd soon as tell the world when she was menstruating. Rita comes up, cheek to a man's I don't know. Not from round here. I would say she is shining.

Why isn't she doing anything? Would you look? I half stand – someone needs to tell these younguns how to parent. He proper pounds his skull, mind. So that's what the hat's for. Helmet, not a hat. Genetics probably, do you need a greater advertisement not to mix? There is an article on the north east. Sunderland was home to such and such who invented the light bulb. How rousing. I'm satisfied with myself that I don't snap at the woman, that I am still able to concentrate.

Next Saturday, I find my usual table in the Wetherspoons. But they're at it again, it's pancakes and beans this time. You've got to worry it might become a habit. Right amount of mess on the floor, on the lad's clothes. Disgraceful. He's huffing like a bull and she's merrily having this cheerful conversation with him. Save your breath, love, I would.

"Would that be nice, Petey? We can have a look and see if they have that song you like. I'll bet they do. What's the one? Happy? Dance? I can't remember, can you?"

The boy has been trying to use a spoon. I mean, why wouldn't she just do it for him? Thousand times quicker. Course everything in it somersaults. He's screaming now. I look about. Nobody's handling the noise well. People come here to relax, for God's sake.

I stoop to retrieve the spoon. Smiling, "Wouldn't waste your breath, love."

And her face looks like I've slapped her. I'm not a violent man. I just like things my way. I smile, trying not to look at the boy, who is woefully messy, and go back to the paper.

"Anoo."

"What'd he say?"

"Ask him yourself."

This requires looking at him directly. All that mess and spittle. "What d'you say, lad?" His throat seems plugged. "Come on, out with it." I shake my head at the girl, expecting some sort of agreement but she raises her eyebrows. Rita did this a lot.

Eventually, I make some sense of the messed up language.

"Did he say thank you?" I pre-empt being told off again. "Did you say thank you?"

Vigorous nodding.

An odd feeling curdles inside me and I retreat to my fry-up. I shake the paper up high. My team's gotta be careful on the next away match.

Saturdays pass. I learn things. Her name is Lisa. She stops a couple of phones from ringing, but always keeps them out, she is always patient and I see her life like a fault on a boiler. Something to puzzle over. And no I didn't mishear, the boy's name's Petey (no, it doesn't fit does it? I imagine it should be something like Mohammed, or Anwar, one of them.) Her relief when I pick something up for them. And I admit, I can admit to this, I admire her, I do. One week, they are not there, and I don't miss them

31

strictly speaking. More feels like when you're about to smile at someone you know, realise it's not them at the last minute. I finish my fry-up, sup my pint, flick the paper, unbothered.

Week after, back, like nothing's happened.
"Missed you last week," I say, easing down. My knees.
"Oh, we just had an appointment."
"Oh very grand. With the Queen?"
She shrugs, slicing up Petey's sausages. "Hospital in London."
"So can they fix him?"
The look on her face is very still – could go one way or the other. And then blossoms into laughter. "No – but – sorry, I've never caught your name."
"Ray."
"I'm afraid we're just trying to find treatment that makes things easier."
"So he'll always be like that? Sorry," I say, though I'm not sure why. "What is it?"
And she tells me the word and pointedly goes back to Petey, who is peering at me when he should be paying attention and eating. His grin, all that drool.
"You should eat, lad. Go on now."
This time, I go to the library and don't look up Rita and her new beau. I Google the word she's given me and the internet fixes it. Just like that. Shame you can't do that with illness, intit. Put the boy into the internet, comes back like you or me. What do the French say when they're happy summat's done? (I put this into the internet an all). *Voilà*. I'll tell Lisa this when I next see her and see what that does to her face. You can't predict her moods. She's a woman, I suppose.
The internet says it's likely that lad'll die in a bit and at

first I feel the relief for her. He won't mind. Shame for him, like, but he's not with it is he? No more conversations for Lisa that Petey can't take part in and then I wonder, no more talking to herself. And then I do think, so whose dinner will she cut up after that?

The next Saturday it's getting rowdy and hot because people like the pub more nearer to Christmas, don't they? They start wearing all those jumpers and parading their families about. There's a group of lads with those pointless Celtic tattoos (they're all from Hartlepool, come on, think about it) and they're pointing at Petey. Doing little shrugs, little spasms – that rolling ball of laughter. I think of a bowling alley, their laughter exploding into each other. The skittles fireworking off.

"Excuse me," I say. "You're being disrespectful."

"Excuse me," one of them echoes.

Another, "Ha yeah, alright old man. We're just having a laugh."

"Can't tell, can he?"

"It's alright, Ray."

"No. Anyone can see the lad's upset. He has this look when he's upset, like when you give him the pancakes before the sausages."

One of the lads says, "sausages," in a deep voice and everybody laughs.

"Do you give him his sausages?" A nudge.

I stand, forgetting my knees. And before I know it, the swell of lads gets all tall and my glasses are off. I'm pitching for them on the floor, going hot. Lisa gives them to me and I shake her hand.

"You watch yourselves, lads," I say. "Not his fault, is it? Them genetics, see. From all that mixing."

And Lisa is not smiling anymore.

"Isn't it?" I say.

33

"We're going now, Ray," she says and Petey waves bye.

I raise my hand.

They don't come back.

Christmas and New Year come and go and I am in the pound shop when I see it, the Timberlake song – Dance. I remember the Saturday Lisa wasn't there. She was going to London, so she would have to go to the train station. I couldn't imagine someone driving her all that way. So I do that. I take my paper and a flask and I read on platform 2 for hours. There's some kids teasing a cat on the platform and I squash the irrational fear kids bring me. I could still beat it out of one at least. That's what canes are for.

"Leave it be, eh!" My voice is louder than I'd anticipated.

They're spiky as they disperse and I burn. I hear something low and laughing. "Yeah alright, granddad."

"No one's granddad," I say, finding the bench again and something feels tight in my throat, actually. My knee is getting worse.

Doctor Pelaw tells me he's seen me sitting in the cold.

"Waiting for a train that never arrives, Ray? Won't do your knee any good out there all day."

"Something like that," but he's already writing a prescription.

"You were there once when I got the train in and then again when I was heading back to Manchester."

I clear my throat. Nod, rest my arms atop the cane. He turns to the computer.

When I do finally see Lisa and Petey at the station, I stand right up, like I'm about to propose.

"What do *you* want?"

Petey is waving, I wave back. "I saw this, I thought he'd – thought you'd like it?" I give him the CD and there is clapping. I nod. "Well."

"Well," she says.

I go back to my routine. Saturdays reading my own paper at my own pace. Fry-up, half pint before noon. And then one day, they are back, just like that. I remember there were pigeons on the roof, and the sky was blue like a cartoon.

"Like to join us?" Lisa says, slicing up Petey's sausages.

The Kettle on the Boat

Vanessa Gebbie

Papa was loading some bags onto our little boat this morning. I asked him where we were going. He said we were going to the other side of the lake.

"Why are we going to the other side of the lake, Papa?" I asked. Papa didn't answer me.

"Why are we going, Papa?"

"Little girls ask too many questions," he said.

Mama was taking down the curtains. There were two cracks in the window. I asked again.

"Mama? Why are we going to the other side of the lake?"

Mama hid her face in the curtains.

I am Qissúnguaq. It is an Inuit name. It means "little piece of wood". I am six years old. I live with my Papa, my Mama and my baby sister. On one side of our house is the sea. On the other side is the lake. This lake is so big I cannot see the other side. In winter the water in the lake freezes as thick as thick. Then the sea freezes. Some men cut blocks of ice and make icehouses.

Once, they cut a block with a fish inside it. The fish looked at me with big eyes. Its mouth was open.

Papa traps animals, cuts their throats and skins them. In the winter the snow is red with blood. He goes out in his boat and catches fish. He guts the fish black red and the birds scream. He hangs the empty fish on wooden gallows in front of our house. They hang there for two weeks. I like to go and visit them, watch their eyes shrivel, dry and fall out. I keep the birds away. When the eyes fall out the fish are ready. Mama cuts them down, dries them and packs them in salt, so we have fish to eat when the ice comes back. For two years there have not been enough fish.

Two summers ago Papa went out to help catch pilot whales. The whales were smooth shiny and black. They made the water boil with froth. Papa trapped the whales and the water in the bay was as red as the snow. I remember it. There are no whales in the bay this year.

Sometimes Papa shoots big geese with his gun. I pull off their feathers and the down flies round the kitchen and tickles my nose, then Mama cooks some meat, dries some on the gallows. The geese have not arrived this year. Papa waited and waited. He had his gun ready behind the door. Now it is too late. They will not come now.

Sometimes there is not enough soup to fill the pan on the stove.

I am on our small boat with Papa, Mama and my baby sister. They don't often take little girls out in boats. It is cold, I am bundled up. My cheeks are frozen. The motor is going put-put-put.

There is a kettle on the boat. It is our kettle from home, the one that goes "hushhhh" when it boils. It is balanced on a cardboard box. I wonder if it has water in. Mama is rubbing her fur boot softly up and down the kettle.

I am glad it is on our boat. That kettle is magic. It fills the room with a big cloud, a warm cloud, and the window gets covered in giant's breath. Mama wipes the glass with her fingers and shows me how to make shapes. When Papa comes back from emptying his traps, the cloud billows outside. It looks like fingers in the air. They mix with his breath then disappear.

Papa is sitting beside me, one hand on the tiller, the other holding my sleeve very tight. I will not fall in, there are not many waves. It is hard to see my Mama's face because she has a hood up. She is opposite me, turned sideways so she is facing Papa, not facing me. She has the kettle near her legs, and my baby sister is on her back in a reindeerskin papoose. I can just see my sister's head. Her eyes are black beads. Black holes in a hood.

It is a long time since I've been out in the boat. It lives in a tin shed next to our house, even in the summer it lives in the tin shed. Papa pulls it up on wooden poles on the ground for it to roll better. I help him rub the weed off it. The weed is green, and the boat is red.

We are going somewhere.

It is a special day. This should be fun, but it does not feel like fun in my belly. I want to ask Mama now where we are going. But Papa is cross, so I don't. Mama is busy with my sister, busy keeping the bags and boxes straight against the rocking of the boat. The curtains are in a bag.

The boat rocks on the lake and I hold on. Papa's hand is tight on my sleeve. He lights a cigarette, a dry old cigarette from a tin under the table. Because it is cold, I can make smoke in the air too, and I blow a white cloud when Papa does. I hope it will make him smile. I have not seen him with a cigarette before. Not in his own mouth. I saw a cigarette when they gave one to the man from over the lake.

We do not have much to give to visitors. We do not often have visitors. We are just me, my Papa, Mama and my sister, some fish in salt and some meat. That's all there is.

The kettle boiled for the visitors. The man and woman from over the lake. The man with the cigarette and the woman with a shawl tied under her chin and no smile. She held my arm and felt it. She said I was strong. When the kettle boiled I could not see them for the cloud.

My mother has a big belly under her coat. She says it is

a stone in her belly. When she says that I laugh.

I see something. I look up and see a big bird in the sky. I pull Papa. I say, "Look Papa! It is a goose!"

It is. It *is* a goose, a big fat goose and it flies round so close I can hear wings pushing the air away. It lands on the lake a little way away from the boat. Mama looks at Papa. He looks at the goose.

I say "Papa? Shall I get the gun and you can shoot the goose for us?"

Papa does not answer. He is watching the sky, and he is sitting up straight. In a while he sits back, and says, "There is only one goose."

I am sleepy with rocking of the boat. I rest against Papa and doze. When I wake up my Mama has the kettle on her lap. I know there is no water in it then. The stone in her belly is pushing the kettle off her knee, but she is holding it there with a mitten. She is holding it to her with one hand on its handle, the other stroking it round.

Now I can see the shore a long way away, and I can see three houses, they are wood. There are no people.

I look at the shore because my Mama is looking at the shore. Then I look back at Mama. She is holding her kettle on her knee, holding it tight with her mittens. She has hunched over it. My sister on her back is wriggling, my Mama shrugs her shoulder to move my sister so she is not bent in the papoose. My Mama is holding the kettle like it might break, holding it gently but steady. She is holding it, hunched over, and her lips are moving.

I cannot hear what she is saying. My ears lean forward to listen but all I hear is the slap slap of lake against the boat, the put-put of the engine, and the whistle of my Papa's breathing.

Something inside me knows something.

"Mama? Is the kettle to go away?"

39

Mama does not answer me. She looks up, a fast look. Even though I am small I can feel this.

It is a special day, the kettle has to go away. Mama is sad.

I look back at the shore. I look at the shore and the houses, no bigger than my little fingernail when I hold up my hands and squint through my fingers at the sun. So I do that. I cover my face with my hands and look at the houses through my fingers. They move around, they are brown birds that will fly up into the grey sky, wheel about and scream.

As the houses get bigger they rock up and down like they are boats. There are two people there now. I do not think for me at that moment. I think for Mama.

The boat comes to the jetty, Papa throws a rope to the man. It is the man from across the lake.

We go up the ladder. Papa and I, we go up the ladder. There is weed on the lower steps. It slips my feet and he holds my hand. He has a bag round his shoulders. At the top I look back into the boat. I wait for Mama, but she does not come. She is not looking at me. She is holding the kettle, looking back over the water.

There is the woman from across the lake. I look up at Papa. I cannot see him properly even though he is close and I can smell his Papa smell.

He gives my hand to the woman. I have mittens on, but her hand is hard, cold. Papa gives the bag to the man.

I say, "Papa…?"

"These people will look after you," he says.

I stand and let the woman hold my hand. I watch my Papa going back down the ladder.

Then I see a shape in the sky! Behind Papa there is another goose in the sky and I shout to him.

But it is not a goose.

And the boat goes away. It does not go back the way we have come. It goes a different way.

There are brown birds here with big beaks. They are screaming over the water. I know, if Papa makes another gallows, and if they hang fish to dry, these brown birds might steal the fish's eyes.

If I am not there to help, how will Mama know when the fish are ready?

The Road to Nowhere

Karen Kendrick

Andy had been driving for nearly seven hours now. The road was quiet today, which was worse when you were tired. The daylight was starting to soften into pink twilight and the lights were flickering on. It was time for a rest.

The city was many miles behind him now, at the end of the long ribbon of virtually identical highway. In front of him was another city. He was in that empty part of the journey where he was surrounded by nothing but road. He couldn't even be sure which country he was in. They all blended into one another after a while. When he reached the city he knew it would look like all of the others; a depot full of trucks and high vis clothing, a van selling snack foods.

He pulled into an empty truck stop by the side of the road, and lay down. Immediately the hypnotic effect of the empty road vanished and his thoughts began to churn wildly.

What if I had a heart attack, here, in the middle of nowhere?

Who would care if I never came back?

I'm getting too old for this. But what else can I do?

He pressed his hands into his eye sockets. He just needed rest. But it was a very long road. He put the radio on, hoping that the sound of another human voice would be enough to calm his mind. He found an English station; they were having a phone in discussion about a van which had been discovered at Calais, full of illegal immigrants. The voice of the caller crackled through the little radio.

'These people... don't be fooled by what the lefty media are telling you. They're not coming in from Aleppo, most of them. They're not fleeing a war torn country. They just want to come here because they know about our benefit system and want to live on easy street. While those of us who work here have to foot the bill.'

The presenter gave a non-committal reply. Andy switched to a classical music station and closed his eyes.

After a moment they opened again, his heart pounding. He was breathless. He knew he was about to have a panic attack. Andy opened the door and climbed out of the cab. The air was cold on his face and his breathing began to return to normal. He began to walk around the lorry, performing his routine checks.

He was checking the back when the banging started. It was unmistakable. There were people in the back of the lorry.

Andy ran back to the cab and picked up his phone. He called the first person he thought of. It rang a few times and then a sleepy voice answered.

'Andy, what's wrong?'

'Listen, Emma, I think there's some people in the back of the truck.'

'What? Andy, what do you mean?'

'I heard banging, and shouting. I'm not taking the piss Emma, it's true. What do I do?'

'God, Andy! How did that happen? When did they get in?'

'It must have been when I was loading it. I left it open. It was only a couple of minutes. God, what do I do? What if they're ill, or one of them's dead? They…'

'Andy, calm down. Listen. They're trapped in the back of your lorry. They can't get to you unless you let them. So this is what you do: I will give you a number for border control. Ring them straight away and tell them what's happened. Then you carry on to Calais and let someone else deal with them. Alright?'

Andy took a deep breath. 'Yes. That's good. That's what I'll do.'

'Right. Now wait a minute.' She paused to search for the number. 'Okay. Here it is.' She read out the number and Andy wrote it down. 'Promise me you'll call right away, Andy.'

'Of course.'

'And ring me to let me know what happens. Preferably in the morning.'

'Right. Yes. Sorry.'

'Bye then. Good luck.'

'Bye. Thanks.'

The phone cut off. Andy stared at it for a moment. He began to put the border control number in and then stopped. He climbed out of the cab and walked to the back of the lorry. At first there was no sound. Andy put his ear to the shutter, which rattled slightly. Immediately the banging and shouting started up again. One word was being repeated again and again: help.

Andy stood back, a hundred thoughts racing through his mind. Then, hands shaking, he began to unfasten the shutter.

'I'm opening it now,' he said. 'Please stay back.' He didn't sound like himself. His voice was thin and trembling.

He pushed the shutter back. Three people looked out at him: two men and a woman. The woman looked like she was in pain.

'Thank you, thank you,' said one of the men. He began helping the woman out of the truck. 'My wife. She's having a baby. Please help.'

Andy stared at the woman. 'No, no, I can't,' he said. 'I don't know what to do. We need to go to a hospital.'

The man looked at the long, open road. 'Is there a hospital near here?'

Andy stared at the road too. 'Not really. I think there's one in the next city. A few hours.'

The man shook his head. 'The baby is coming now. Please help us.'

Andy felt trapped. What could he do? He went back to the cab and took out his coat. He placed it on the floor. 'There. She can, er, sit down.'

The man looked a bit confused but he gestured to his wife to sit. She gave a low moan and didn't move. She began to speak rapid words in another language. The man placed his hands on her shoulders and spoke to her softly.

She was only young, and very frightened. Andy wished he was somebody else, anybody but himself. What could he do to help, a forty year old bachelor?

'I'll call someone,' he said. The man shook his head.

'They won't be able to get here quickly enough. And then they'll send us back to Syria. Please. You don't know what we've been through. You must help.'

'Right.' Andy frowned, deep in thought. 'But if we ring someone, maybe they can tell us what to do. Like NHS direct or something.'

The man shook his head. 'She'll be OK. My friend here was training to be a doctor before the war. He'll help.'

The woman began to walk up and down alongside the lorry. Every few minutes she would stop and howl with pain.

'I have some whiskey in the cab,' said Andy. 'It might take the edge off the pain.'

The man smiled. 'No, thank you. It's not permitted for us. But you're a kind man. What is your name?'

'I'm Andy.'

'I'm Firas,' said the man. 'My wife is Amira and my friend is Ammar.'

Andy ran his hands through his hair, one of his nervous

45

habits. 'This is a really strange situation for me,' he said. 'I mean I want to help and everything, but I could get arrested if I let you stay in the truck. I could go to prison.'

Firas placed a hand on his shoulder. 'If you knew what we had been through you would help us. I'm sorry to trouble you like this. But I need to get my family to a safe place. The house we lived in no longer exists, it was destroyed. You would have done the same thing.'

Andy thought about his small terrace, levelled by a mortar bomb but the thought was cartoonish, ridiculous. He could hear Emma speaking sternly in his head. *Don't get involved. It isn't your problem Andy. You have to follow the law.*

The woman gave a loud scream and began to babble and cry in her own language.

'It won't be long, now,' called Ammar.

Andy walked to the other side of the truck and sat down. Firas followed him.

'Are you alright?' he asked.

'Me? Yes, I'm fine. I just, well, it's private. I feel a bit awkward.'

Firas laughed. 'Me too. Ammar knows what he's doing. Let's leave them to it.'

'You speak good English,' Andy said.

'I went to Leeds University,' replied Firas. 'BSc Mechanical Engineering. I was hoping to use my skills to help make my country great. We're going back to Leeds, if we can make it that far.'

Andy said nothing. The feeling of panic was growing inside his chest again.

They sat in silence for a while. 'Do you have any cigarettes?' asked Firas, eventually. Andy shook his head.

'Don't smoke. Sorry.'

'Neither do I, normally,' replied Firas.

Ammar began to shout. He sounded worried.

'What's he saying?' asked Andy.

'He needs our help,' replied Firas. 'Come on.'

Andy followed him around the truck worriedly. Amira was lying on his coat, extremely distressed. The other two men began a conversation in rapid Arabic. After a moment Firas turned back to Andy.

'The baby is stuck. It's in the wrong position. So we have to try to get it out. Come on. We must help.'

Andy stared at him open mouthed, then glanced at Amira. 'What can I do?' he asked, swallowing.

Firas and Ammar had a quick discussion. 'Please can you try to find something we can use to wash? Or some gloves? Do you have anything like that?'

Andy went back to the cab. He sometimes kept antibacterial gel in the cab. He found it straight away and was about to go back when his mobile began to ring. It was Emma. Andy stared at it for a moment and then decided to ignore it. A few moments later he received a message:

Can't sleep for thinking about your situation. Ring me for an update pls. Em. x

Andy's stomach turned over. He switched the phone off and returned to the others.

'Here,' he said, handing over the gel. 'It's all I have, sorry.'

Ammar smothered his hands in gel. 'Thank-you,' he said. Andy nodded. Amira screamed.

Andy walked away, feeling entirely useless. He sat in his cab, fiddling with the radio restlessly.

The minutes ticked by slowly. Andy felt like an anxious relative in a hospital waiting room. He longed to go back outside.

Finally Firas tapped on his window. He looked worried.

'My son has been born,' he said. 'But Amira is bleeding.

We have no choice. We're going to have to take her to a hospital.'

'Right.' Andy couldn't help it; he felt relieved that the decision had been taken from him. Then that feeling was replaced by sudden panic: what if she died, in his truck? He left the cab and walked back around. He could hear the baby's first shrill cries cutting through the silence of the night.

As he approached Ammar held out the small bundle to him.

'This is my son, Mohamed Wassim Andy Nasry,' said Firas.

Andy laughed. 'No, you don't need to do that, I haven't helped at all really.'

Ammar was trying to hand the baby over to him but he stepped back. 'No, I'm fine, really.'

'Please,' said Firas, smiling. 'If you hold my son, we'll help Amira.'

Andy took the tiny bundle and held it uncomfortably. He looked at the little scrunched up face and wondered what kind of life this child was going to have.

'I'd like to help you,' he said to the baby. 'But it's out of my hands now, anyway.' He turned to Firas. 'You may as well sit up front now,' he said. 'I have a sort of bed at the back of the cab. Your wife can lie on that.' He worried that it wasn't very clean. But it was better than nothing, he supposed.

The road seemed even longer now, the city further away.

'How is she?' Andy asked, after a while.

Firas spoke to Ammar and then turned back to Andy. 'She is losing blood quickly,' he said. 'How far is the hospital?'

Andy looked at the satnav. 'Half an hour, traffic permitting,' he said.

48

Everything else had faded into the background. Nothing mattered now apart from to get this woman to a hospital before it was too late.

Finally the truck pulled into the hospital car park. Andy pulled over as close to the door as possible and hurried over to the desk.

'Can you help me please? She's bleeding, she's had a baby. Please help, she's in my truck.'

The receptionist looked at Andy like he was crazy. *I sound like a madman*, he thought.

'What name is it?' she asked, in a thick accent.

'I... I don't know. Please, it's an emergency. She's in my truck.'

The woman went to speak to somebody and a moment later two paramedics appeared with a stretcher. Andy breathed out.

The last time Andy saw Firas and his family was when Amira was being carried into the hospital. Firas was carrying his son in his arms.

'Well, goodbye,' said Andy.

'Thank you,' said Firas. 'If you hadn't opened the truck she would have died, and probably my son too. You are a kind man.'

Andy didn't know how to reply so he just nodded.

'I hope you find somewhere safe to live,' he said.

'Me too,' said Firas. Then he and his family were gone.

When Andy got back to the cab he picked up his phone.

'Andy. What's happening?'

He took a deep breath.

'I was wrong,' he said. 'There was no one in there. One of the barrels had got loose and was rattling about, that's all.'

There was silence on the line.

'Are you serious, Andy?' said Emma, after a moment.

'I've been awake half the night because you didn't secure the goods properly? Bloody hell, Andy.'

Andy put the phone on speaker and began the final leg of his journey. The sun was beginning to rise.

'Sorry Emma,' Andy said, smiling at the phone as Emma continued to complain.

Home

Vanessa Harbour

It's happening again.

Twenty-eight pairs of eyes turned to stare. Taking in everything about us. Assessing our 'coolness'…or not in my case thought Daisy.

At least she wasn't alone this time. Daisy sneaked a look at the other girl, who wore a scarf wrapped around her head, and noted with a sigh that the girl hadn't been forced to stand there in every bit of uniform on the school list, right down to a flowing grey cloak. Unlike her. It's Dad's way of helping her fit in or that's what he always told her. Mum didn't approve. It didn't help, it made her look stupid. While she walked to class she'd noticed there wasn't one cloak on any of the pegs. The list was a lie and she felt ridiculous. She wondered if the girl would like to swap parents. She's got hardly any uniform and Daisy had more than enough. She could share.

"Class, I'd like you to welcome Liliane and Daisy, they're both starting our class, 6B, today."

Liliane, Daisy noticed, barely looked up. There must've been something very interesting on the floor. She hadn't said a word since they'd come from reception and the head teacher Mrs Jenkin's office either. Daisy had tried to be friendly. She'd thought, as newbies, they should stick together. Liliane wasn't having it. Daisy hated starting new schools. Sighing deeply again, she prayed maybe this would be the last time and perhaps just once they could stay here for a while. She was tired of 'starting afresh.' Five new schools were enough for anyone. Mr Taylor, whose glasses hung on the tip of his nose, had been rabbiting on. She knew she should've been listening; however, she'd switched off.

That's one of her problems see, not listening.

"Grace, I'd like you to help Liliane settle in, and Sophie, you can look after Daisy." A girl with perfect blonde hair rolled her eyes as her friend with matching hair nudged her. There were four of them around the table, all with matching hair styles. Great, she thought, I've been put with the cool gang. This was not going to be an easy start.

Grace's dark hair hung in two very long plaits down her back; she pointed to a seat next to her and smiled at Liliane, who sat down beside her saying nothing. Liliane had beautiful dark eyes. Daisy was desperate to know her story. A weight of sadness hung about her.

Daisy plonked herself down in the spare chair next to Sophie, who just nodded before continuing to play with her perfectly matching pink pens, pencils and pencil case.

Why do my parents do this to me, wondered Daisy, making me start a new school in the middle of term. I hate it. It's the worst thing ever. Nobody ever wants to be your friend. She pulled out her mismatched pens and pencils all held together in her Snoopy pencil case. It had lots of stains on it but she didn't care.

"What's that?" asked Sophie poking at it.

"Snoopy, he's my hero." Daisy stroked the image.

"Whatever! I'm Emily, that's Holly and she's Freya. We're the best," pointing to the others. Her clone friends giggled before bombarding Daisy.

"Where have you come from? You're not from round here? Where do you live?"

"Leighton Buzzard."

"Leighton what – don't be stupid no one lives in place called that," said Holly flicking her hair back.

Daisy sighed again and looked at all the posters on the wall. Why did all schools look the same? Posters on maths, nature and the Victorians seemed to be stuck to all walls.

"Where do you live now?" Emily had a purple set of pens and pencils just like Sophie's pink set.

"We've moved into the vicarage." Daisy pulled her hair out of her scunchie, she could hide behind it then as it fell into a long dark curtain.

"OMG! Your dad's the vicar." They started to roll around in their chairs laughing.

Here we go. "Actually my mum is. My dad's a writer," Daisy muttered.

They laughed even more, thumping each other. "Don't be stupid! WOMEN can't be vicars."

Looking down she swallowed hard. Daisy was not going to let them get to her, not on her first day. She wondered if Liliane wanted to swap places. Peeking through her fringe Daisy looked over to where she sat; Liliane looked as miserable and alone as Daisy felt.

Daisy survived the morning, saying nothing and doing exactly what she was told.

Tapping hard on the table with a white board pen, attracting everyone's attention, Mr Taylor started to speak again. His voice sounded very deep. "Grace, Sophie, make sure you look after Liliane and Daisy during lunchtime. Make sure they know where to go and what to do. It's your responsibility."

"Oh great!" grumbled Sophie next to me, "I've got to babysit. Come on then."

Daisy trailed behind as they led her towards the dining hall, which was actually the main hall as she found out later. The clatter of plates and cutlery echoed around the walls. A smell of school dinners wafted out. It was curry today. Liliane and Grace were in front of them. Grace showed Liliane what to do and where to go. Daisy watched her plaits bounce on her back while she walked along. Liliane almost smiled as she listened intently.

53

"Watch this, it's a good laugh!" giggled Emily. She moved forward and grabbed hold of Grace's plaits giving them a sharp tug backwards before shaking them, shouting, "Come on, giddy up. Be my horse. Just like yours. Let's go for a ride."

The clones laughed, shouting "Giddy up" too. Daisy stepped away.

Grace snatched her plaits away, her face puce and twisted with anger. "Get off!" She led Liliane away quickly.

Sophie looked at Daisy, her mean eyes sparkling. "What's the matter with you? Why aren't you laughing? That's funny. Come on, you have to come with us to have your lunch, baby."

Daisy really didn't want to be here. She didn't want to be with them. What could she do? That joke wasn't funny. She didn't like it. Perhaps I could convince Dad to home school me, thought Daisy. She looked around and bit hard down on her lip to stop the tears that threatened to overflow. Not now, please not now.

The following day she was back at school. Dad hadn't listened insisting she went back. He'd told her it's only first day nerves and she's being silly. Sometimes she wished they'd hear what she was really saying but they were always too busy; Dad being creative and Mum's always too busy listening to other people to hear what she had to say. So that's how come she found herself standing outside the school again facing another day. Feeling really alone.

As Daisy took a deep sigh she heard a kerfuffle to one side. Looking across she saw some of the boys had got hold of Liliane's backpack throwing it around, not letting her get it back. Snatching it. Pushing her. Teasing her. That wasn't on.

Luckily Daisy's quite big for her age, which was a

distinct advantage in this situation. She stomped right into the middle and pushed over Alfie pulling the bag off him as he fell backwards.

"That's not yours. Give it to me!" He was too shocked by the surprise attack to put up much of a fight. The others stood askance.

"Oi!" shouted Jake, "You can't do that!"

Daisy looked at him and raised an eyebrow, "You really think you can say that?" She had one hand on her hip, before she marched over to Liliane. Handing over the blue, slightly battered backpack she asked, "Would you like to walk in together?"

Liliane looked up very briefly, half smiling and nodded. She whispered, "Thank you."

When Daisy got into the classroom Liliane went and sat with Grace. Daisy had to face sitting with Sophie and the clones again. She braced herself and walked towards their table. They all had matching hair bobbles today, in their appropriate colours of course. Sophie's was pink, Emily was purple. Holly was orange and Freya was green.

"We saw what you did? What was that about? Why did you help HER?" You don't know where she's come from? She doesn't belong here?" Sophie poked at Daisy with one of her pink pencils.

Daisy didn't reply and sat down with a thud. Her dad was wrong. It wasn't first day nerves. This place was full of horrible people.

Mr Taylor bounced in, his glasses still on the end of his nose with a very bright yellow tie poking above his sweater. "Class, I've some exciting news. There's going to be a brilliant assembly coming up this week. Something to really look forward to but I'm not going to tell you what it is because it's a surprise."

The whole class groaned. "What's the point in telling

us, if he's not going to tell us what it was?" muttered Daisy.

"You needn't groan. I wanted to tell you because I want you to be on your best behaviour in the meantime. That means being kind to others." He stared pointedly at the boys and then at Sophie and her clones.

"What's he staring at me for?" complained Sophie, flicking her pencils, "Don't know what his problem is? He's picking on me. I'm going to tell my mum."

I bet her mum is one of the governors or on the PTA thought Daisy, always the type my mum would say. She'd know how to deal with her. Daisy got lost in one of her dreams. Wondering what the surprise might be. Mr Taylor had said it's exciting, but of course, as her mind wandered, what Mr Taylor thought was exciting and what she thought were exciting might be very different. She drifted off and let the images of as many exciting things come into her head. She thought of a snowball fight, a puppy, going to the beach or having a new computer game were all really exciting. However, would Mr Taylor think they were exciting things too? It's only when Mr Taylor clapped his hands to announce lunchtime that Daisy realised she hadn't done any of her work. She'd be in trouble.

At lunchtime Sophie and her clones surrounded Daisy.

"We've got some exciting news," declared Sophie. Daisy wondered if she could cope with this much excitement. "We've decided you can be in our gang. But to be in our gang you have to do two things. One you have to have a colour and all your pens and pencils etc. have to be that colour. Also your hair bobbles have to be that colour. Right?"

The others smirked.

Daisy shrugged. She wasn't sure if she was supposed to be flattered.

Emily carried on, "The colour you've got is…brown!"

She smiled the brightest and sweetest of smiles as if this was a wonderful thing. All the other others did the same thing trying to stop their shoulders shaking.

"Secondly, you have to do an initiation," Sophie struggled to say it but no one dared laugh at her, "test, like the grown up gangs do." Sophie suddenly looking very serious. "You have to go and tell Liliane she needs to go back to where she belongs and get out of our country."

Daisy gasped then quietly said, "Thank you I like brown, it's one of my favourite colours." All the girls looked a little aghast. It wasn't an answer they expected. "I'm not changing my Snoopy pencil case though. It's my favourite and my nanny gave it to me. I'll have to think about your initiation test though." She didn't give them time to speak as she got up and walked away as fast as she could; going straight to the girl's toilets. A film of sweat forming on her face and down her back. Her heart pounding. She looked in the mirror, her face was white. Resting her head against the mirror she let its coolness help calm her down. The sound of her heart stopped thrashing in her ears slowly. She stayed in the loos, hiding in a cubicle, until the end of lunchtime. How could anyone be so nasty?

Luckily when they went back into the classroom they were put into their Math's sets and Daisy was in a higher set than all the clones so she didn't have to face them all again that day.

The following day was meant to be the day of the special assembly which still no one had any idea about. On her way into school Daisy had bumped into Liliane as she came along the road.

"Can I walk with you please, Liliane? I'm not sure I can face going there again today." Liliane looked at Daisy her brow furrowed. "Everyone is so horrid. I've been to so many different schools and have never met so many nasty people. And my mum and dad won't listen." Suddenly the feelings of totally unhappiness and loneliness overwhelmed Daisy. She burst into tears. Great heaving sobs wracked her body. Liliane pulled Daisy into a hug and held her tight, whispering quietly.

"It's okay, we can be friends."

"Please, that would be wonderful," Daisy hiccupped. She was tired of being brave.

"We better go though because we're going to be late." Liliane handed Daisy an embroidered handkerchief, "Here wipe your tears. You've got a really red nose now." She grinned.

"I always do when I cry. I hate it; I always look like Rudolf the Red Nose Reindeer." Daisy stopped, "Do you know about Rudolf?"

"Sort of. Come on." She pulled Daisy into the playground.

Stood there in a line waiting for them though were Sophie and the clones. They all had their hands on their hips. They surrounded Daisy and Liliane, pushing and poking at them.

"Ah I see you've made your decision Daisy O'Keefe. I better send the message then hadn't I?" she shouted.

A crowd of adults, including a very old man, stopped behind them and watched. "Liliane Adjmi, you and your lot are not welcome here. Go back where you come from. Go home. We don't want you lot." She then spat straight in Liliane's face before they ran off towards the classroom, all the clones laughed and cheered with her. Doing high fives as they went.

Daisy gasped, taking the hankie, she gently wiped the globule of spit off Liliane's face. Tears ran down both girls' faces. Neither spoke, both too shocked. The adults, who had been watching, raced over; one of them was Mr Taylor and another, in fact, was Daisy's mum.

"Oh Daisy, I'm sorry I didn't believe you when you said this was going on, I thought you were being silly."

"Girls, they will be punished, don't you worry. They will not get away with this. Are you all right?" said Mr Taylor, "Not quite the welcome I would like you to have had to our school. We're not all like that I can assure you."

Both girls nodded, a little shakily.

The old man stepped forward and took Liliane's hand, "I'm Herbert Horwitz, I'm ashamed to say, I'm that horrible girl Sophie's, great grandfather. She'll be punished at home as well. I can assure you. I'm so sorry Liliane. I actually know a bit about you as Mr Taylor has been explaining. I wondered if you would also do me a favour. Perhaps I could explain as we go along. It's a bit cold for me to stand out here for long. I'm well over eighty now and am not too good at standing for long." The old man smiled. His eyes twinkled and creased at the side. Daisy noticed how his hair was so white it looked like a cloud.

"Gosh, yes of course, how thoughtless of me," said Mr Taylor, he put his arm round the back of Mr Horowitz and guided him towards the building. "I better go and sort the class out too. Daisy and Liliane, would you go with the Revd O'Keefe and Mr Horwitz into Reception please? The head teacher will sort you all out."

Daisy felt very confused now. It'd been a horrible morning so far. Mum hadn't mentioned anything about coming into school. Mrs Jenkins, the head teacher, gave both Liliane and Daisy biscuits and squash to drink while they sorted out the assembly. It seems they were both a couple of heroes for some unknown reason. Daisy wasn't quite sure why. She didn't feel like one though she did like the biscuits. They were chocolate. The only time she'd been in Mrs Jenkin's office properly had been when they'd come to see her about Daisy starting at the school. It was very neat and very blue probably because the school uniform was mainly blue seemed the logical answer to Daisy. There was a vase full of bright yellow daffodils in one corner. She decided it looked like the sun in a blue sky.

Mr Horwitz took Liliane to one side and explained what he wanted her to do. She smiled when she came back. A proper, really big smile. The first one Daisy had ever seen her do.

Soon they were all taken into the main hall.

"Daisy," whispered Mum, "you can sit with me so you can see everything. I've got to go up and say something first then I'll be back with you in a moment. "

Daisy didn't mind what her mum did as long as she didn't have to sit with Sophie and her gang. She took her place at the side of the stage. The whole school came in and sat on the floor in front. Daisy could pick out Sophie and her clones quite easily.

Mrs Jenkins introduced Daisy's mum who stepped onto the stage.

Daisy could see Sophie smirking and laughing with the clones.

"It is such a joy to be here today. It is one of my first events as I start in my new job here. It is always difficult starting afresh." Oh no, here we go thought Daisy. Don't start talking about that. She started to cringe as her mum went on. "It is really hard to start a new job or start a new school. Having to make new friends. I think this time though we'll be here a while." Daisy's mum briefly looked across at her, half smiled giving her a nod. Daisy knew what it was code for. Perhaps they would get to stay for a change. Revd O'Keefe looked back at the expectant faces. "Today, is a special day, I'd like to introduce you to someone, who was the first person to welcome me in to the community, and who opened his heart to me, quickly becoming a good friend. I've asked him here today because I want him to tell you his extraordinary story of how he came to live in Britain. Mr Horowitz..." She turned towards the old man with his cloud hair. "I'll let you explain."

Daisy noticed Sophie's mouth drop wide open and her face paled. Daisy however sat up straight and felt a bubble of pride grow inside as her mum stepped off the stage and joined her.

Mr Horowitz shuffled to the front of the platform. He had a slight hunchback.

"My name is Herbert Horowitz and in 1939 I was part of the Kindertransport. Do any of you know what it was?" Sophie's arm immediately shot up. "No Sophie I'm not asking you." Daisy could hear her irritated huff from where she sat. Mr Horowitz spent an interesting and shocking half an hour explaining what it'd been like living under the Nazis and why his family had made the decision to send him to Britain on his own. He ended with "This means I'm a refugee and I want to introduce you to another refugee."

At which point Liliane stepped from behind the stage and again Daisy could hear Sophie's gasp. Mr Horowitz continued, "I'd like you to meet my friend, Liliane Adjmi. Do you know Adjmi means free man? You heard about my journey to Britain and how dangerous it was, but if you want to hear about danger you should hear about Liliane's journey. She's very kindly agreed to tell you about it." He squeezed her hand and smiled at her.

Liliane stepped forward. She looked round at Daisy, who also smiled and nodded at her. She looked very pale and was visibly shaking. Daisy noticed Sophie begin to nudge her friends and point, before Liliane had a chance to notice Daisy stepped up on stage and stood by her side.

Briefly taking her hand and squeezing it. She whispered "You can do this."

Mr Horowitz looked at them both and nodded, "Yes you can, you've been through far worse. Don't let them win."

For a moment Liliane closed her eyes and took a deep breath then she started, "Today I was told I should go back to where I came from, I should go home." Everyone gasped and Sophie dropped her head. "Trouble is, here is my home now. I lived in Syria. It was a really happy place until the war started and they started dropping bombs. Then it became so scary. I lived in Aleppo. It's been on the news. One night the bombs came and they landed on our house." Liliane's looked down, she gulped. "I managed to crawl out but..." Focusing on the back of the room, Daisy could see her eyes were full of tears. "My parents didn't. They were killed. It was horrible. Distant cousins came, who I didn't really know but they were they only family I had left." She wrung her hands over and over nervously. "They decided it would be safer if they got me out. See I don't have a home to go back to there.

"We travelled in the back of lorries, on boats, we walked lots until my feet really hurt but we couldn't stop." She continued to describe the desperate journey they had, how frightened she felt particularly when some people had hit her. Liliane thought she would die. But they got to the 'jungle' in Calais. There were lots of people there. She told them all how freezing cold and wet it was there. Then like Mr Horowitz good things had happened she had ended up with a foster family in the UK who are looking after her even though she's a refugee. "They're really kind. I've a home" Liliane smiled.

At this point Mr Horowitz stepped forward, putting his arm around Liliane, "That's the best thing about the people in Britain, they care about others. They never turn their back on people who need their help. They never say cruel things or threaten to send people back."

Daisy could see him staring at his great granddaughter who looked at the floor. Her friends were staring at her. "Refugees are welcome in Britain. The world is made up of global citizens. How it should be now. It makes it a better world."

Everyone started to clap and Liliane put her arm around her new friend.

Daisy had a feeling from now onwards she would be all right in this new school. She felt at home.

Boarding House

Debz Hobbs-Wyatt

Stay as long as you need

The sign reads: *Always open.*

A man sits outside. He looks up from the shade of a tree; his back pressed against the trunk. He has a notebook in his hand. He seems familiar but you can't be sure.

It hangs crooked, the sign. Crooked on a red front door. You hesitate for a moment before you knock. Knuckles to wood. The man does not react; his face lifted upwards, as if contemplating the sky. Now the door swings open: a smell. Not a bad smell. More a *can't quite place it, feels like home* kind of smell. Like apple pie. Cinnamon. Spices. Like a memory so far away you can barely hold onto it. You feel the weight of your weather-beaten backpack nag at your bad shoulder; feel it slip. So now your faded denim hangs crooked, like the sign. You readjust, prop the backpack into place and nudge the door some more.

This is it. You're here. But you don't remember how you got here; or why you're here.

Just as you don't remember your name.

It started with a song. It was a soft, sweet lullaby of a song. And the scent. *Her* scent – a pink flowery powdery kind of scent. It twirls in circles around her. She didn't know you could feel smells. Or see them. Just as you can feel colours. Mama taught her that.

This scent is like a peck of softly planted kisses, like tickly rose petals. It feels pink.

But it isn't real… is it?

None of it is.

64

It's all gone.

All she has now is *the room. This room.*

They gave her the yellow daisy room. *Perfect for a little girl* Miss Maya said. She wanted to tell her she isn't a little girl; not anymore. She will soon be a woman. When she makes babies of her own she promises she'll keep *hers* safe. She doesn't think she can make babies yet; but when she is old enough... she doesn't know if it's allowed; it doesn't say it in the rules. *How do you even make a baby?*

The rules are everywhere; written on signs – like the one on the front door, only that isn't really one of the rules. Everyone is welcome, no one is turned away.

The sign written over the front door reads: *'Rule #1: Stay as long as you need.'*

The rules are on plaques and they hang on hooks on doors and behind doors; and on walls and in cupboards. There's even one in the toilet. Miss Maya says there are ten in all. When the time is right, she says, you will find them all, Milka, and then you will understand.

Yes she says. Yes. I will understand, Miss Maya.

She doesn't say how she doesn't like rules.

How one day she broke a rule.

And look what happened.

So all Milka has now is this room. And a view she has never seen because she never opens the curtains. She tells Miss Maya she will do it when she's ready. Miss Maya never tries to change her mind. All she does is smile. *When you're ready, Milka. All in good time, Milka. You will do it, Milka.*

But what if she doesn't?

Milka pulls the edges of the yellow duvet around her small shoulders. She hides her face in the pillow that smells like home and thinks about her mama's sweet perfume and how one day when she's big and strong she will be able to open the curtains. She thinks about the cat, the feel of its fur. The cat visits every day. It's a Persian cat. White. She misses her when she doesn't come. She hasn't come today.

As she closes her eyes she thinks she hears the door downstairs creak open; footsteps marching on the wooden floor in the hallway; she even thinks she hears Miss Maya's voice. She always talks quiet but she knows the tone. Someone new is here.

She wonders if Miss Maya has asked the question yet, they always ask the question.

Milka wants the new one to be Mama – sometimes she rushes to see, but the pad of the feet tell her boots; a man's boots. Mama would never wear a man's boots. She wonders what he'll say when she asks him the question.

What is your gift, Milka?

I don't know, Miss Maya.

You will.

Now she sinks deeper into the yellow and dreams of home before the war came… she wonders what colour he is, the new one, if he has olive skin like hers. Does he know her language? Except there is only one language here; no barriers. That's how Miss Maya says it: no barriers, Milka. And one time she added, *only the ones you build around yourself.*

Maybe the new one has black skin – like the preacher. She wonders if she can trust him – not the preacher, the new one. She wonders until sleep finally steals her away.

The woman stands in front of you.

She wears a long white dress and brown leather sandals. Old, worn; well *oldish*, her body not her sandals. The bend of her spine says she's old, white hair frames her face, but no lines and she has smiling eyes. They remind you of someone. They're blue. You don't know who. She asks you something you don't quite catch so now she is looking at you like she is waiting for you to say something. When you don't she offers to take your backpack. "You're hurt?" she says.

"No. Well yeah, maybe."

"I'll carry it."

"No, it's okay."

"Here."

"No."

You add, "Sorry, I didn't mean to—"

"It's okay. It's really okay Tom."

"Tom?"

"Welcome."

"Did you say Tom?"

"Let me show you the way, Tom."

You follow her; the pad of heavy black boots on wood, backpack digs in, you feel the pain in your neck, across your shoulders but somehow you like the pain. You don't know why. You wonder if you can smell something – incense? And you are sure you hear something – music, chanting from behind one of the doors; a man's voice.

Her dress flows behind her as she walks and her bare toes go click-clack in those sandals. The walls are wooden panels, lines of photographs in metal frames; faces you don't know. *Or do you?*

They watch you. And so does she. "You're at the front, top of the stairs, third door on the right…"

Is she waiting for you to do something?

Maybe she means for you to go there.

You wait.

"This way," she finally says. "It's okay. Let me show you, Tom."

So you follow. A sign reads '*Rule #2: Always, always be kind.*' You read it twice. Light comes in from a window on the landing. Dust angels float, like wedges cut out in the light. You like the way the light does that. You used to paint. They're enchanting these dust angels. Someone called them that… your grandmother; the one from Coney Island? You don't recall her name. Didn't she have blue eyes? Or was it someone else – someone younger?

Miss Maya she said her name was; not your grandmother from Coney Island or the someone younger, the woman in the white dress and the click-clacking sandals with the quiet voice. The one with the long white hair, who is now standing in front of an open doorway. The music; the soft laments come from a door across the hallway. A door half-open. She doesn't mention it so nor do you.

"Your room, Tom," she says.

She says the doors are always left open; unless you want to be alone, and then you close them. Otherwise it means you are open to visitors. She says it's one of the unwritten rules. It doesn't have a number.

"Oh." You have never stayed anywhere like this.

The room is blue; like the sky: walls, carpet, bedding. All blue.

"Relaxing," she whispers, as if she hears your thoughts. "It's what you need, Tom. It quietens the mind."

You stare at the window; a blue curtain flaps in a breeze where the outside comes in. You think maybe you should ask what happens next and what about food and—

You never heard her leave.

She left the door open.

Now you hear something else; above the chanting; someone singing; it's a more familiar sound; the melodic tones of a piano. It's a ballad… a man's voice you are sure you know; a song so familiar you are certain you know those beats, so moving – but you can't hold onto them and now they're gone.

So here you are, Tom. You have arrived. Checked in at the boarding house. But you still don't know why you're here.

You will find out soon enough. Perhaps a 'visitor' will tell you.

So you slowly sit and ease your backpack onto the large blue duvet. Now you tug at the zipper. You slide out the photograph and hold it between your fingers. You know it's something you have done many times. It's a black and white picture. All you know is you loved her and the baby she holds in her arms. You loved them but you don't know what happened, just that they aren't here and you haven't seen them for a long time. So you lay the photograph face down on the bed. You wish you remembered. Or maybe it's better this way.

And just like that you let go.

Your sobs drown out the screaming inside your head. And the chanting from across the hallway.

It's the bell.

The tinkly sound of the dinner bell. It floats to her; wakes her but at first she pulls the duvet tighter and closes her eyes harder; searching – searching for her mama's face in the shapes. The bell comes again. Miss Maya says she has to eat. When she first came here she never did. Miss Maya would bring trays of all her favourites to her room. She'd never told her they were her favourites. Then one day she had felt the weight of the bed dip; felt the heat against her legs. Miss Maya? "You have to eat, Milka, you have to stay strong." But she was sure it was her mama's voice she heard. When she opened her eyes no one was there. Except for the white cat.

She has eaten every day since except for the day she was sick and she thought she would die but she didn't. The day the preacher came. And the woman from the end room was there too she thinks; the pretty one; the actress, or so Miss Maya says. The one the cat belongs to. The cat was there all the time when she was sick. She has seen the actress in the lounge; she always seems so sad. Not like an actress or maybe she is acting she's sad and if she is then she is a great actress. She dines with him – in her room since he came – that other man. He's the important one. The American one. The suited one.

Milka knows she has to go down and eat because that's when she will see the new one; if he comes. They don't always come – the new ones. Not at first; some not for a long time. They don't always leave their room or leave the door open, or… is he safe? The new one… will he hurt her?

The third bell.

So now she is pushing the duvet off her legs; kicking it off the way she did for Mama, playfully, and then she is standing and looking at the pulled across curtains, before she is skipping into the hallway and making for the dining room and wondering some more about the new arrival. Maybe he will have seen her mama? Maybe he will know something. Someone must? But how does she know if she can trust him? How did you know which ones are on your side?

He is white.

He is big; not fat big (not like some of them) but muscly big.

And he is white or better he is pink. Not yellowish like the chanting man, the monk, in the red and orange robes. They say white when they mean pink, don't they. She is pink: pale pink – the American actress and her important friend, they are 'the pink Americans'. She smiles when she thinks that. She likes to amuse herself when she doesn't know their names.

The new one is standing in the doorway looking in like he doesn't know why – or what the bell means, like he doesn't know it's dinner time. Like he's half way in and half way out and he's got stuck. Miss Maya says lots of people are like that; they get stuck. But he did come, didn't he. He came when the bell went. Maybe it's an instinct; like those dogs who salivate to bells but don't know why. She learned it in science. Miss Maya says the man outside is a scientist: she calls him the English scientist.

Miss Maya will show the new one where to sit; if he can't decide. So Milka waits her turn but Miss Maya doesn't come yet. She thinks she should say something; but she doesn't. Not at first. Instead she stands and she waits and then she thinks about the third rule: the one that's up in the dining room on the far wall in big bold letters. It reads: *'Rule #3: Do at least one good thing every day.'* So now she steps closer, praying softly under her breath; and now her hand is lightly brushing his; big hands. Like her papa's. She mustn't think about that. She thinks she wants to pull away but she doesn't. *Do at least one good thing every day, Milka.* Even this. Yes even this, with the strange man.

He seems to tense; his whole body twitches and now she can feel his tremble; like a buzz, like the cat's purr so she slides her hand deeper into his big, wet, clammy hand. And she holds on; holds his hand still, gently, ever so gently squeezing it the way Mama used to do if she was afraid… to stop the tremble. *Please be on my side. Please don't hurt me.*

"Do you want to sit with me?" she whispers.

When he doesn't answer she takes one step forward and pulls. It's a nudge, a gentle tug, a soft tease but still he doesn't move – maybe he *is* stuck. So she tries again. This time she feels him wield to her. So now she shuffles; leads him slowly across the bare wooden boards, him in his boots (her with bare feet) to the table in the corner; away from the window, the one she always chooses. He follows and now they stand, hand in hand and stare at the white tablecloth, two small glasses; two white coffee cups and two white dinner plates; two sets of everything. Miss Maya must have planned it this way. That's when she starts to let go but as she does she feels his hand squeeze hers back, ever so softly and she realises there are tears on his cheeks. She teases her hand free and gestures to the seat. "Here," she says. "I always sit here. So you can sit there, opposite me. Okay? This for you. I saved it for Mama but you can have it for now."

She's not sure what she sees in his face. But he nods.

He eases the chair out.

He sits. The light catches the tears and they glint.

He's wearing a T-shirt. It's plain. Black. Faded blue jeans. The boots. She can see the bulge of his muscular arms. She looks at his big hands. He wears a gold wedding band. His hair is tousled; curly. Brown. Handsome she thinks. She wonders why he cries but she doesn't ask.

He looks around. It's like he is afraid to look at her; at first. But when he finally does she sees the tears have dried and she finds his kindness; right there – just in the place Mama always said it should be. *If they're a good person, Milka, you will see it in the eyes. But be careful, Milka because some people are not what they seem.* Is he not what he seems, should she have taken his hand? *But if they're kind, Milka – you will always see that; even if they're broken.*

Broken.

Was *he* broken?

72

Is *she?*

Miss Maya says everyone gets broken sometimes.

She sucks in a deep breath. "Don't be sad," she whispers. "It's gonna be okay." And then she adds, "I'm Milka."

But all he does is look down at his hands, twisting the gold band around his finger and he doesn't say his name.

You met her at dinner.

A young girl, maybe twelve? She is called Milka. She's from Croatia Miss Maya said when she came later with some hot tea. You think about Milka as you lay on top of the blue duvet; your boots neatly lined up against the wall, your backpack under the bed; the photograph on top of your pillow. You think how the baby in the picture got to twelve; or was it thirteen? You had forgotten the way a hand could feel in yours.

You hadn't realised you were crying; not at first. Nor had you realised how hungry you were until Miss Maya served your favourite: chicken stew and biscuits (like your grandmother used to make, comfort food, day trips to Coney Island in the fall and then whole summers). Once you started eating you couldn't stop. You only realised you had gravy on your chin when you looked up to see Milka's young face. You didn't understand the gesture at first; she had wiped her finger across her chin, looked at you imploringly with those big brown eyes. She did it three times until you picked up your napkin and mirrored her action. That's when she smiled; giggled, threw back her head. You had a good friend in the army whose family were originally from somewhere like that, in eastern Europe. You see his face when you think of hers; for a moment, you try to think of his name, hold his face for as long as you can until it's gone. Like him. That terrible war. And now your hands tremble and you close your eyes and make it all disappear. In the end you forgot what the fighting was about.

Milka.

You hear her name as you drift out of your doze.

Milka.

Such an unusual name.

Milka – who seemed as if she wanted to ask you questions. A few times mid scoop of her rice and she would look and open her lips as if the words wanted to come but then didn't and she satisfied herself with another mouthful. Maybe she wanted to ask your name. She did ask one thing; right after you'd finished your cream pie while she picked at the skin of an orange, too big for her delicate hands. She looked right at you and she said, "Are you a soldier?"

She popped a segment of orange into her mouth and her head dropped ever so slightly to one side. Poised; waiting for you to speak. So you laid your spoon down in your dish and looked right at her and you told her, "I was."

"American?"

"Yeah."

She seemed to think about that for a long time before she said, "Were you in the war? Did you see my mama?"

"Who's your mama?"

"She's so beautiful. Maybe you saw her. You would remember if you saw her. That's how beautiful she is. Like that actress."

"What actress?"

"Only the actress has blonde hair."

"What actress?"

"The glamourous one – everyone loves her."

So then silence except for the sounds of her sucking on her orange and you didn't know what to say but you

74

couldn't leave it with her looking at you like that.

"Well? Did you see her? My mama? Did she send you?"

"Why would she, I mean I—"

She watched as you chased the last of your cream pie around your dish with the spoon and you said, "I might have, I don't really remember things, I—"

Maybe you did? And just as you finished the last mouthful, you said, "My wife was like that."

"Like what?"

"So beautiful you would never forget her."

"What was her name?"

She looked at you so intently you felt the need to look away; view the others you'd heard come into the dining room. You were sure you knew the one by the window, a guitar propped against the wall; speaking to the other one in the small round glasses. Arguing about music or something. You were sure you knew their faces. Finally you looked back at Milka. "She had blue eyes."

"Oh. I have brown."

"Yes – you must take after your mama," you added. "Such a pretty face."

And that's when she smiled.

That's when she unfolded her hands, wiped the juice off her fingers with her napkin and when she whispered, "I hope so." Slowly she nudged back the chair and stood up, one hand on the white tablecloth. "So you'll help me, then, you'll help me find her?"

You looked at her; how could you resist that smile? But… but how will you help her? It has been such a long time and… but you said it anyway, didn't you. You looked right at her and you said, "Yeah, okay. I'll try"

"Promise?"

And maybe you shouldn't have said it but you did. You said, "Yeah. I promise."

75

And she'd clapped her dainty hands together and turned and she even seemed to skip across the dining room. But at the door she turned and looked back. "I'll come and find you," she said. "Leave your door open."

Before you had time to respond and were wondering if you had done the right thing you saw Miss Maya. She was standing watching from the corner of the dining room and she was smiling.

The sign reads 'Rule #4: Help those who cannot help themselves.'

Milka reads it now as she stands in the library staring at the old man. She has seen him before.

Last night Milka dreamed how the new one was going to help her. They would prove Mama wasn't dead; not like all the others, not like her papa. The man said he had been a soldier. And he's on the good side but she doesn't know what is good and what is bad anymore. But he said he would help her, didn't he – so he must be on the good side. She had dreams and dreams are important. Someone taught her that. But dreams, memories: sometimes they all get mixed up in the same place so you don't know what's real in the end, do you?

She was up before the first bell; dressed (in her denim jeans and her fairies T-shirt) and she was ready. She heard clinking sounds from the kitchens, smelled coffee brewing and bread baking.

But *he* was not at breakfast.

She'd waited it out watching them all come in, one by one – even the black preacher man was there this morning. Miss Maya had been folding napkins and watching and she wanted to ask about the American soldier – but she never said anything. Milka knew better.

And now his door is closed. She had wanted to knock but Miss Maya said if there is one rule you *have* to follow it's that one and maybe it ought to be Rule #1 and not Rule #5: it's the one that's in every room. The one that reads: '*Rule #5: Always respect other people's wishes.*'

So now Milka stands in the library glancing at the old man at the far table; he is wearing a grey suit and he has a grey beard and a grey moustache. She might have seen him before but she has never spoken to him. She watches as he looks along a line of books and then glances over in her direction.

"We all have a story," he says, "our past makes us who we are."

She looks at him, stood there, his face all serious and she thinks about her story; about home and about the dog that used to come to her yard; a stray that adopted them. Black. She has not thought about him in a long time. All she knows is they had to leave it all behind. Run they said. Before they get you.

She wonders what happened to the black dog.

"Dogs have good instincts."

Miss Maya says he's very clever; a 'type of doctor' she said. But how did he know what she was thinking? How—

"The dog will be fine; I'm sure, Milka. Dogs are very resourceful."

And how does he know her name? Did Miss Maya tell him?

"I hope so," she whispers, running the edge of her finger lightly along the dark wooden edge of the table, creeping closer towards him. But the others are all dead. She wonders if he was buried in the rubble too: the dog – like Papa – and then she pushes the thought away.

"What's your story then?" he says.

Nothing comes. Nothing. Absolutely nothing.

"No matter," he finally says, turning back to the bookshelf.

"I think I'm lost," she whispers. There she's said it. Although she had practised saying it to the soldier with the big hands but now she has said it to the old 'type of doctor' man. And she wonders if she really meant to. That's when he turns back to look at her. He seems to look along the bridge of his nose as if he's wearing glasses; but he isn't. Not today. He smells of cigars. She knows this smell. Grandpapa smoked them but that was so long ago.

"Is that so?" He adds, "Sit." Like she's a dog. She pulls out the chair and complies.

"What makes you think you're lost?"

"Miss Maya says lots of people who come here are lost."

He does not sit but looks at her, tapping a pen against the table.

"Or they ran away, and there is nowhere else to go."

He nods.

"She says it's safe here. For everyone. No one is turned away."

"It is safe, Milka."

There is a serious look on his face; but a softness in the way she speaks.

"So tell me about you, Milka."

"I don't think I'm really lost."

"Oh?"

"I think I'm missing."

So now he drags the chair out so she hears it scrape, wood to wood, and he sits slowly, and looks right at her.

"The soldier said he could help me find my mama."

"I see. Sounds to me, if you're missing, that she is the one who has to find you."

"You think? But how will she know where to find me?"

78

"Sometimes you need to go back to the beginning to work it out."

"You do?"

He has an accent like hers.

"What happened to you Milka?" he says. "What's your story?"

You don't know how long you stay in your room; standing at the window watching the man sat under the tree. He has something in his hands today; something he moves through his fingers – looks like glass. He looks like he is trying to catch the sun.

You have been thinking about Milka, your offer to help. But what if you can't help her? What if you fail? You have failed before. But you made a promise didn't you?

Are you a coward, Tom?

The photograph is in a frame – you think Miss Maya did that. When you returned from dinner one night there they were: looking out at you from the bedside table. And now all you do is lay still and look – or stand up and look – and you try to remember. All you know for sure is that what happened to them was something bad; something so terrible you had to shut it away.

You look back at the man outside; see him adjust the position of the glass in his hand like he is really trying to do something. And that's when you turn back to the bed and think some more about Milka. You want to help, but what if you can't?

More time is lost; you don't know if it's morning or afternoon. All you know is it's still light outside and the man is still out there. You're watching from the window again. You see him tilt the glass between his fingers and just like that you see a rainbow arc across the square of grass under the tree. You see the way the light is bent into colours and reflect off the man's face who is smiling a half-smile, like the thing he was seeking he has found, but not all of it, like he is still trying to figure something out. The colours are so beautiful, so truly beautiful you want to hold this moment in your hands; you want to tell your wife (Susie, yes Susie, her name is Susie) and your daughter (what is her name, come on Tom what is her name?) and you want to say *come look at this, look how magical this is... like an angel's wings* and for a moment you want to paint it, to capture the colours and... but you can't, can you? You stopped painting, didn't you? Just like you stopped believing in angels.

You stare at the photograph in the frame.

You can't help Milka, can you? You're a coward aren't you, Tom.

You think how sometimes things happen and there is nothing you can do.

That's when you look at the door; a lip of white light bleeds along the edges – and you wonder – if you keep it closed will anyone find you? You have had this thought before. It was another room; an apartment in upstate New York. No wooden floors; a grey carpet with coffee stains that looked like blood. A closed door behind two closed doors. No chanting but a TV someplace; sirens from the street below. A half-drunk bottle of whisky.

And a notion.

A notion that some battles you can never win.

A notion that *this* was the only way.

It would be three days before anyone came.

Do you remember what you did yet, Tom?

Milka has never told anyone about being missing before or about how Mama said she had to run or they would come. She had run, but she'd got herself lost and now in her sleep

80

she still hears her mama calling out to her.

He tells her he is Jewish; this 'kind of doctor' with the soft voice who smells of cigars. He says he comes from the Ukraine. Then he says that he knows about wars – he says there are many kinds of wars. He urges her to continue.

But she doesn't know how to find the words; or make him see that they did everything they were told, but still nowhere was safe. Mama said keep running; even if we are separated keep running – all the way to the border. And she did, but did she even know who she was really running from and what the fighting was about?

The monk told her, not long after she came here, that what the world needed was love. "More peacemakers, more healers, more lovers. It should be about love," he said. And the last thing, the thing that she still remembers. He had looked right at her; said, "You have a good heart, Milka. Use your love."

Maybe that was her gift? But when she asked Miss Maya all she said was, "You will know when you know."

Rule number 6 is in the library. It's on the wall by the door as you come in. Milka looks over and reads it now while the 'kind of doctor' talks about the final solution but she doesn't know what he means, just that he says he is glad not to have been a part of it. The sign reads: '*Rule #6: Embrace your differences.*'

"The biggest wars, Milka," she hears, as if he can see inside her, but he mustn't see what she saw, she doesn't want him to see… "are the ones that happen right inside your own head."

"Oh."

"Those are the most dangerous battles of all."

"Yes," she whispers. But how can she tell him what she saw, and how she kept running and people said her mama was dead but she didn't see her body. She never dug *her* out of the rubble. And now she thinks about the screaming and the sounds of the bombs squealing in the sky and... no.

No.

Shut it all away.

And they're wrong about Mama. She is still alive.

She looks away, but she won't go near the window, can't go out there. But just like that, in this moment, she sees something. But it can't be, can it? She sees a rainbow where the light hits the glass and thinks for a second that she is here with her: Mama. She always said rainbows are signs from heaven. Like angels.

Milka went missing because she went outside.

She hears the doctor speak again.

"I can help you," he says. "But you have to tell me what happened."

She looks at him.

"We are here to help one another Milka and I will help you, *moj mali anđeo* – my little angel."

Her lips part, how did he... Mama used to say that to her every night.

And she utters one word, one tiny little word as the colours dance on the walls. "Yes."

You find the sign in the wardrobe, hanging there – and you have been staring at it for the past ten minutes. Or it might be longer. '*Rule #7: Love without condition.*'

And you did; always. The way your grandmother (the only one you knew), the one from Coney Island, the way she did. The way she loved you – didn't she. Even when your dad was in the state penitentiary and you would never end up like him or your mom. She taught you how to love, didn't see, your grandmother. She made apple pie with cinnamon and spices. She took you to the church. You learned about love and you loved them, Susie and—

You did. You did with every part of you.

You couldn't wait to come home; you were a good soldier, weren't you. You couldn't wait to see them, could you? Couldn't wait to tell them how much you loved them. You'd had enough of hate; enough of fighting. Enough. And you were going to tell them that too, weren't you.

But you never saw them, did you?

So where are they, Tom?

Haven't you remembered yet, Tom?

The doctor does not write anything down.

He watches Milka the whole time; nodding in all the right places. Even when she said how her papa's body was in the rubble; how she had dug out his hand. And the worst part – the part only she knows. The part she has never said. The part that makes her feel as if she is falling inside her own head and she will never stop until she clatters to the ground. She tells him that he was holding someone's hand when they found him. Two grey hands in the rubble dust with their fingers entwined. It's the image inside all the bad dreams.

It happened so fast.

The bomb.

The shouting.

The running.

The dust falling around them in the silence.

And now the sobs she can't make stop.

He is sliding a box of tissues across the table towards her. He lets her do all the talking and she has never talked like this. How her papa had died trying to save someone else – she doesn't know who, just that it makes him a hero.

And now she tells him how she had to keep running.

83

Run and don't let them get you Mama said. Only she ran so far her mama can't find her.

She watches the doctor's face. It has been fifteen minutes and she has run out of new things to tell him.

"Mama isn't dead. She can't be. She is out there somewhere – trying to find me."

She has lost count of how many times she has said this.

He nods again and this time she sees his eyes shift to the open doorway where Miss Maya is standing. That's when she sees that the actress has come into the library. She is in a beautiful white dress and her hair is so... she doesn't even know a word better than beautiful. She is in the 'History' section and Milka hears the man speak and the actress laughs. It's the first time she has heard her laugh. She is even more beautiful when she does that.

"So do you feel better?"

Milka turns back to the doctor. She wants to answer him but she doesn't know if she feels better. She doesn't know what to say. So instead she looks again at the Americans.

"Milka, you did very well today. Thank you for sharing you story. It has been a terrible thing that has happened but none of it is your fault, you understand that, don't you? War takes many lives."

But she knows it is her fault... if she hadn't gone outside then...

"Milka, I am always here. When you need to tell me more."

"But there isn't more to tell."

With that he slowly lifts himself from the chair, says something about needing a smoke but he will be in the library every day when she needs to speak to him. And now she watches him leave. He looks at the American man and for the first time Milka sees his face, she thinks she knows

84

it but she can't be sure and then she sees the doctor smile at him, "Mr President," he says, tipping his head. "Don't forget your session later." But before Milka has time to think about what he sees Miss Maya is speaking to the doctor in the doorway but she isn't smiling. She looks serious. Too serious. So serious Milka wonders if she did the right thing telling him what happened.

You have not come out of your room for three days and while the rule is to be left alone if the door is closed, Miss Maya is allowed to come in. She doesn't tell you it's a rule but you think it must be, maybe another one of the unwritten ones. She knocked ever so softly and she poked her head in, bringing in the light, and the dust angels and all she said was, "I am leaving you a tray of food. And these."

She left without saying what 'these' were and you still haven't looked – have you?

Or eaten the sandwiches even though you can smell the pastrami on rye – can't you. Your favourite.

You look at the photograph of them, Susie and Claire – her name came to you in the middle of the night. Claire. She had green eyes not blue like her mother's. Green like yours. But far worse came, didn't it, Tom, and that's why you have shut yourself away, even though you know the girl – Milka – has been and gone many times. You have heard the quiet patter of her footsteps and seen the shadow run along the bottom of the door. One time, might have been this morning, you even heard the monk chanting out there. Like he was casting some kind of spell on you. Maybe to make the bad dreams stop.

You used to take pills for that. Don't you remember?

And that dark place is back – and the song. The ballad. Twice you've heard it today.

You look across at Susie holding Claire as a baby and

you try to see her face at thirteen but it doesn't stay and now you're sobbing again and you're sure someone is outside.

What did you do, Tom?

At first you hear Miss Maya and then you think someone else, a man but you can't be sure of anything, so you bury your head in the blue duvet, wonder if you will ever know what really happened and why one fall afternoon in your apartment building, you did what you did.

Coward.

So where are you now Tom? Have you worked it out yet?

The door opens and Miss Maya and a man with a grey beard and moustache come in.

"You didn't touch your sandwich," Miss Maya says. "Or your paintbrushes. I left you some canvases there too."

"Paintbrushes?"

"There's someone you need to talk to," she says. "Urgently. I will leave him with you."

Did she say paintbrushes?

All you can think now is how you want to paint.

"I can help you," the man says. Then he adds, "My name is Sigmund."

Milka is back to the library, she is watching the actress. She has such a glow these days, like she is the not the same person; not the same actress who never left her room when Milka first came here. First time she saw her she was crying in the kitchen asking had anyone seen her cat; she said she's even asked the man under the tree. She said he was rude. Had looked up, as if he was thinking and he might know something and then he had said, "No." Just like that: "No." And then she said as she was coming back inside he had added, "I cannot calculate the madness of people."

"What was he saying? I am mad. Well I told him *you're the crazy one, honey*," she'd said. "Who does he think he is?"

That's when Milka said, "I think I know where it is."

"Where what is, sweetie?"

"Your cat. It visits me."

"She does?"

"Well then, she must really like you, honey."

"I've been thinking about Rule number 8," the actress says to Milka now.

"Rule number 8?"

She is even more beautiful this close up. Such blue eyes.

"Rule #8," she says, "is the one that says: *'put other's needs before your own'*."

"Oh."

"So I was thinking," she says, red lips shaped like a kiss. "You will mind Mitsou for me, won't you?"

The white cat? But she loves that cat...

"Are you going somewhere?"

"I think you need her more than me, right now – so you'll do that for me won't you?"

She says yes but she doesn't know if she should. What her mama will say when she comes. She never liked the black dog.

"It's okay, Milka. When you don't need her she'll come back to me, okay?"

"Won't you miss her?"

"Sure, but I have the dogs."

She doesn't remember dogs; maybe she left them at home. She would remember the dogs. She likes the dogs. But she loves that cat.

"Can't we share the cat?"

"I have to go home soon, Milka."

"Oh."

"So we have a deal?"

"Yes. Okay. Thank you Miss—"

But all she does is bend down, her face is level with hers and now Milka thinks she needs another word for beautiful. She smells the way the cat does when she presses her face into the fur. Not like her mama's perfume, this is darker, but she loves it all the same. The actress presses her red lips to Milka's cheek. She is sure she has left her pout there. "That's settled then."

"Yes."

Milka watches as she walks away but then she stops, turns back. "You will take good care of her, won't you, honey?"

"Promise."

And that's when Milka thinks she should have asked when she's checking out but it's too late. She watches the door close behind her.

Mitsou is already purring on her bed when she goes back to her room five minutes later.

You still don't know what happened. Not yet.

All you know is that the doctor spoke to you. He said it will take time; but you can take as much time as you need; that there are lots of people here who will help you.

"Yeah," is all you said. "Yeah." Just one word. "Yeah." Like that.

And then he'd pointed at the paintbrushes and the canvas. "I heard you used to be pretty good."

You don't know how he knows this.

"So maybe that will help you?"

You followed his gaze.

"Express yourself."

"Yeah." There's that word again.

88

"Sometimes we have to go back to the beginning to find ourselves again. Go back to your happy memories, Tom."

You'd thought about Coney Island.

Then you heard him say that he'd be back, same time every day.

And just before he left he looked right at you and said, "Maybe you should leave the door open, in case she comes?"

You were about to ask who, in case who comes, when he added, "You made her a promise."

So are you really a coward, Tom? Or are you gonna keep that promise to Milka?

Miss Maya is standing in the hallway with a feather duster.

"What's my gift?" Milka says. "I still don't know, Miss Maya."

Miss Maya smiles. "You will."

"Does it have to be something you can see or hold?"

"Like what?"

She sees her shake out the feathers in her duster.

"Like a thing? Like a cat?"

"No." She smiles.

"Oh."

She thinks some more.

"Is it something you do? Like act, or sing or preach or heal?"

"Very good, Milka. It can be."

She thinks about that for a while, twirling a loop of hair around her finger. "But I don't do any of those things."

"You can do many things, Milka."

Now Miss Maya is already half way out of the room when Milka sees the black preacher. He is standing by the door. He runs his finger long his moustache and his eyes widen. "Milka," he says. There is a smile in his voice.

So that makes her steps closer towards him. "Yes?"

"Did you see this?"

She follows his gaze to the sign on the inside of the front door. Rule number 9.

"No. I never saw that one before." But she has never been this close to the door before.

She reads the words: *'Rule #9: The time is always right to do what is right.'*

"But I don't—"

She sees him looking at her; really looking at her. "The time has come."

"For what?"

"The time has come to do what is right."

"Oh?"

"It's time to go outside, Milka."

"No!"

No way. No, no no.

"It's too dangerous, I can't—"

She leans away from the door; pictures Mama when she told her to stay inside; keep the curtains pulled, hide. And about what happened last time, the one time she broke the rules and now she is lost and Papa is dead.

"Open the curtains, Milka. It's the only way to see what's there."

"No. Mama says—"

She sees the way he smiles; the whiteness of his teeth, she sees his kindness. But she mustn't go outside. She knows she can trust him, he is the one who taught her is the good to have a dream but—

"Milka."

"Yes?"

"You know what you can do?"

"No sir?"

"You can help him understand by being the best of whatever you are."

What does he mean? The best of who she is? And help who… but she thinks she already knows.

His words dance in her head long after he leaves the room.

You have been here for days. You have been lying on this bed and listening to this chanting and looking at this picture.

Milka hasn't been for a while; maybe she doesn't know the door is open – though it is only open enough for the light to get in.

You painted something yesterday. A man. In a grey suit. A bit like the doctor who speaks with you every day. You painted him. With an apple over his face. You remember seeing that painting on the cover of a magazine. It's famous. You don't know why you painted that. You never really liked it, did you? But he did; the doctor. He loved it. Well, it was a start. Today you will try to draw the dust angels, the light. Your grandmother showed you how to paint – remember? She said it was a gift. Your gift. She took you to the galleries in New York. You used the painting to help you deal with what happened to your dad; and your mom when she was drinking and they had to take her away. Remember?

Thank God for Susie.

Didn't she say your paintings were wonderful and why weren't you painting anymore?

You never told her how could you? Not after all the terrible things you saw in the war. How could you find beauty in anything again?

You think about the rainbow.

You look at the photograph of Susie and Claire.

You think how you would like to paint *them*.

Claire needs to be older. Claire is thirteen.

91

They were going on a trip.
Weren't they flying someplace?
Where?
Try to remember, Tom. You need to remember.

You don't remember getting off the bed, only that you can feel the weight of the brush in between your fingers long before you start to paint. You can feel the colour, someone told you could do that; feel colour. Wasn't it Milka?

You need to capture the way the light comes in; the dust angels. That's what you need to do. So now you pull the curtains as far across as you can and you see the man in the garden. Maybe Milka will come today.

But what will you tell her?

That you did something bad?

That you're a coward?

The doctor says she needs to go outside; she needs fresh air. He says maybe you both do. He said you need to find a way to make Milka go outside. Maybe that's how you can help her find her mama.

Milka is standing in the doorway looking at the American soldier. Finally the door is open. She has left Mitsou on her bed.

Her soldier is painting.

He is painting the window and the way the light comes in and it's like… beautiful.

She doesn't say anything. All she does is watch. He seems different. More relaxed somehow; like he's lost in it but it's a good kind of lost.

She doesn't know how long she stands here before he spots her.

"Milka."

"That's like… amazing."

"You think?"

"Maybe you can draw my cat?"

"You have a cat?"

"A borrowed cat."

"Oh. Yeah. Sure."

"Why does this man have an apple in front of his face?"

"Oh. That one." His eyes move to where it's propped against the bed. "Not sure."

"Oh."

"Will you ask the man outside something for me?" "Can't you?"

"Ask him if he has any apples?"

Why would she ask such a silly thing?

"Will you go outside and ask?"

"No. I can't I—"

And now she sees he has picked up the paintbrush and is staring hard at the canvas. It seems he has forgotten the question. She has lost him again.

When she goes back to her room Milka wraps herself in the yellow duvet and buries her face in the cat's white fur. She won't go outside. We won't talk to the crazy man under the tree. She wants Mama more than she has ever wanted her but what if she never finds her? And then she thinks about her American: what if he never helps her? And she thinks, anyway she hates apples, she only likes oranges.

Time has no edges; not like the paintings.

You can't hold it in your hands. Time is meaningless. Some days you feel as if you have not seen Susie or Claire for years; and other days it feels like moments. You can't hold their memories, sure you can reach out and grasp them – but they don't stay for long. They float past; like clouds. You can't hold onto clouds either, can you? You have been

93

trying to think of all the things you can't hold in your hands. Like hopes and dreams and wishes and… memories.

Claire was good at science; you remember that. She was a grade A student.

And Susie was… everything. She was everything. Everything. That's all you can think about. Susie. Was. Everything. You met her at high school; you knew you would marry her from the moment you saw those blue eyes. Your grandmother loved her. You have to draw them: Susie and Claire. The doctor said it was a great idea. You want to draw Claire's face at thirteen, but can you remember it?

Can you remember it when it stopped? When time stopped. Just. Like. That.

Do you remember when they told you what happened?

And just like that you know who told you. Your grandmother from Coney Island; she was sobbing into the phone.

It was something bad; something *really* bad. Something so bad you have lost the memory. Lost it; let it float away like a cloud. Now it's missing.

What was it, Tom?

You can't hold onto it. Just like you can't hold music in your hands either, can you? Like that song, you imagine all the things in the song. Good things. You make images in your head to chase away the bad things. The doctor says sometimes we do that to protect ourselves. We bury our memories when something is too hard to deal with, so the trick is figuring out how to unlock it.

He tells you about Milka. You didn't think doctors were allowed to do that, talk about other patients but he says she isn't a patient. She's another guest.

And then he'd thought and not said anything for a long time before he smiled. It was a real smile, you'd not seen that before and he'd laughed too, "I figured it out."

94

"What?"

"The way to help Milka."

"You did? Go outside you said?"

"Yes but first you need to help her remember."

"Remember what?"

"Ask her why she held your hand in the dining room."

You'd crunched your eyes up, shifted position on the bed, your neck was hurting. You wanted to say wasn't she just being kind? Wasn't that why she held your hand?

But time slipped away again, didn't it, because by the time you looked up and then down from the window you saw him in the yard talking to the man. Both were looking up at the sky, it's like *he* is still trying to figure something out, not the doctor, the other one.

Maybe that's what we all do. Maybe we're all trying to figure things out.

Their heads were both tilted; watching the curl of the doctor's cigar smoke as it drifted skyward.

Milka has one rule left to find. She doesn't know what her gift is. She still hasn't opened the curtains.

But something has happened.

She doesn't know what but she feels it; deep inside. She knows she feels different and yesterday Miss Maya kept looking at her and after dinner she saw her carrying clean sheets and now she wonders if someone new is coming and maybe it's Mama.

She knows the actress has gone home; and sometimes it works like that, someone leaves and a new one comes. The important American man is still here though and lots of people were talking to him in the library yesterday. The black preacher talks to him a lot and it looks like they make secret plans.

She sensed the something happening when she woke up

and Mitsou wasn't on the bed and she still hasn't seen her. The doctor says cats are very intuitive too, that's a word he likes. He told her the other day – when she found him in the library. He asked her if she was ready to tell him the rest of the story yet, and she said there was nothing else to tell.

"Is that so?"

"Yes."

"The soldier, he's your friend, isn't he?"

"Yes."

"Good."

Then he'd nodded and said he had things to do. Important things. "The solution," he said, and she'd hoped he wasn't talking about 'the final' one again, "is always the thing that's right in front of your nose the whole time. Like apples."

"Have you seen my cat?"

"The one you asked me to paint?"

"She's gone."

Milka stands in the doorway. Her feet are bare. You hoped she would come today because you have been thinking about what the doctor said.

"I have an idea," you say.

"An idea where my cat is?"

"No. Not that."

"Oh."

"She'll turn up."

"It's just—"

"Just?"

She stays in the doorway; doesn't come inside.

"I never got to say goodbye."

You study her face when she says that.

"I never said goodbye to Mama. Or Papa."

A memory comes loose, like a bubble that shakes and

then it's gone. You think something like that happened to you.

But what she asks next makes you stare at the photograph by your bed. You didn't expect her to ask that, did you? And you don't know the answer anymore.

What she says is, "Why do we have wars?"

Now you're afraid of the dark place and so you move closer to the window. Closer to the light.

She has that look again, like you have all the answers. Like you can make everything alright.

You shake your head.

"But you're a soldier. You must know?"

"I followed orders."

"Like rules?"

"Yeah. But sometimes... sometimes I do try to imagine a world where there's no war."

She lowers her gaze, plays with her hands. "Me too."

"Come here," he says. You see her look at the window.

She shakes her head. "Not the window."

"Milka?"

"I can't."

"But I want to ask you something."

Before she responds, before you can ask her, you both hear it.

A squeal.

A scream.

Now Milka has her hands on her ears and you think for a second she plans to run.

"No, it's okay Milka. It's really okay."

You look down – it's only the squeal of a cat and the scream of a man. And the cat is in the tree and rattling the branches and you see what's happened. It seems the cat has knocked off an apple and the man under the tree is rubbing his head, staring at the apple he now holds in his hands. And the odd part – it seems his scream is not one of pain because he's laughing. Actually laughing.

"Come and see this, Milka!"

"No."

"Your cat is outside!"

"Mitsou? Outside? But it's not safe outside."

"Come on."

"I can't."

"Come and look."

"No."

"Then let's go outside."

She follows slowly behind you, you see Rule #2 on the wall and you see the photos in their metal frames, you know these faces. And... is that Claire? She was there all along? Aged thirteen. Claire is on the wall? So now you stumble and you feel the weight of your boots trip you and you feel the wood come up to meet your knees and now... now you feel Milka's hand push gently into yours, like she did that day when you first came and she's asking if you're okay. But you don't know, do you. You don't know if you're okay.

And now you wonder who is helping who.

The front door stands open at the end of the hallway.

Milka still has her hand in yours but this time it's you pulling, teasing, urging Milka to step towards the door; to where the outside comes in. You have to not think about that photo, but at least now you have a way to remember when you paint Claire's face. Somewhere you can hear Miss Maya's voice and is that the doctor? Perhaps it's coming from the library. And there's that song again. It goes round in your head, over and over, like it's stuck on a loop. It was playing that day, don't you remember now?

You had it on repeat.

They found you in your apartment.

You had been there three days.

Behind the closet door.

There were lots of flies but you wouldn't have seen that would you?

They had to cut you down.

You feel the pain come again in your shoulder, your neck and you know what you did now, don't you. They played the song at the service, didn't they?

You need to go outside. You can't breathe. Outside. You need to... what you really need to do is think of her now and not you. To help Milka. You have to; you made a promise, didn't you.

You push the memory of that day away.

But as you do you hear Susie's voice – you're sure it's her, but the moment is so small it flutters away but you're sure she says, "You're not a coward, Tom, you were never that."

"Come on," you whisper. "Come on, Milka. We'll do it together. Hold my hand."

And that's when you know. That's when you realise. Right as she squeezes your hand and you see the man dancing with his apple; that's when you know.

Maybe you won't know it tomorrow; maybe you won't know it in five minutes. But right now you know; you know everything. And you know you have to help Milka.

Things fall.

Lots of things fall, you fell, the apple fell – but so did they.

We all fall down; even your grandmother said it. *We all fall down, Tom, but what counts is that you get back up.*

They fell out of the sky. That's what happened to Susie and Claire.

It was September. They were coming to meet you...
because they couldn't wait, could they. They couldn't wait.
She had something to tell you, about the clinic, about the
last time you came home – and you'd guessed, hadn't you?
You'd guessed she was having another baby but she wanted
to tell you. They were coming to you when it happened.
They couldn't wait.

The plane hit the tower.

Everyone fell.

Everyone fell out of the sky over New York that day. It
was the day it rained terror.

That's what happened.

Dust and rubble.

That's what the wars were about.

And now you're stumbling again but Milka still has a
hold of your hand.

She is crying. Like she knows what happened to you but
she can't know that.

It's a moment later you see the real reason *she's* crying.

Someone is standing behind the tree. And Milka is
saying one word, she is saying it over and over and over –
the way that song played.

She is saying, "Papa."

She remembers.

She knows what happened. She knows whose hand her
papa was holding in the rubble. He came to look for her;
she'd gone outside because she wanted to look for the dog.

"Milka!" he'd called out to her.

"Papa? I saw him, the dog, he went this way."

"Milka."

"This way, it was him, I swear."

"Milka."

She'd stopped.

He'd run towards her. "Leave the dog, he'll be okay."

That's when it happened.

That's when the bomb went off.

He reached her just in time. And she knows now. It was her hand he was holding when they died.

Is it over yet? Milka leans into Miss Maya, she sits and Milka leans her body into her and lets Miss Maya play with one of her curls. She says Papa is waiting in the yard, she'll see him from her window, he'll still be there when she's packed her things.

"Where's the cat?"

"Oh animals have a way of showing up where they're needed Milka."

"Like the black dog?"

"Him too."

"So where's Mama?"

"She has things to do, a life to live."

"So she's not dead? So I *was* right."

"You were right."

Milka thinks for a bit then.

"Can my soldier leave yet?"

"He still has a lot of work to do, Milka, before he's ready to leave and be with—"

She stops twirling Milka's hair and looks into her eyes.

"You mean the ones in the paintings, don't you... his wife and daughter and he said there was to be another baby."

"Yes that's right."

"But he will be with them?"

"Of course."

"Just like one day I'll be with Mama."

She feels the warmth of Miss Maya's hand fold over hers. "Yes Milka." She adds, "Now hadn't you best go get ready. Don't keep him waiting."

"Miss Maya?"

"Yes?"

"But what is my gift?"

"You have many gifts, Milka. Look how you helped the soldier."

"Many?"

"You didn't know if he was good or bad did you. But you trusted your instincts. And you showed great courage. Courage is a wonderful gift, Milka, that sits up there with your kindness."

"Courage?"

She stands straight, twisting her hand so it now sits in Miss Maya's.

"The doctor says you did well, he'll be outside when you go, he's reacquainting with your papa."

"He knows him?"

"Of course. He was looking for you for a long time when he was here – but you weren't ready to see him."

"Oh."

Miss Maya squeezes her hand.

"Miss Maya, what's Rule number 10?"

"You'll find it behind the curtain, Milka. On the window."

"It's been there the whole time?"

"Yes, Milka. But you can only see it when you're ready."

Miss Maya now lets go of Milka's hand and she looks into her eyes before she turns and runs to the door, her bare feet pitter-pattering on the wooden boards. At the door she stops, looks down, opens her hand. She sees a white feather on her palm.

She's gone. Milka. She's gone.

You saw her go. You were standing at the window and

you saw her go. She came to you to say goodbye and to tell you she had opened the curtain and read the last rule.

"You opened the curtain?"

"Yes."

"And what did the rule say?"

"I mustn't tell."

"Oh."

"So you painted them?" She looks at the canvases propped against the blue wall.

"Yeah."

"They're so beautiful."

"Yeah."

"So, you know I have to go now…"

You feel your heart tear when she says that. "This is for you," you say.

You lift the canvas from the bed and hand her the painting, you watch her as she studies her own face there, next to it a white cat… you hope you have captured the likeness, you only saw the cat for a moment.

You think she might cry. Milka says she promised Miss Maya she'd be strong. She promised she wouldn't cry, but you see her wipe her eye on the sleeve of her jacket.

"Will you keep it for me," she whispers.

"You don't like it?"

"No. I love it. I more than love it – but you need a way to remember me when I leave. This way you will."

You don't know what to say and the next minute she presses her lips to your cheek. "How does it feel?" she says. "The kiss."

"Like… a rose."

"Tickly?"

"Yeah."

"What colour?"

"Pink."

103

She smiles.

"Oh," she says. "About Rule number 10..."

"Yeah?"

"Miss Maya says she will let me tell you at the right time. So... well... it says '*You must forgive yourself'.*" She adds, "Maybe that will help you."

You think about that, you stand and you think about that a lot before you tell her, "I would never forget that pretty face, Milka."

Then she's gone.

Milka skips into the hallway, across the wooden boards and looks along the row of faces all lined up in metal frames. She reads some of the names; Miss Maya says everyone is there; some stay for a long time, forever if they still have things to do. Those singers are there; they all have their names underneath: one of them just says *The King*. She prefers the music the other one sings, the one with the little round glasses because he said it was good to imagine a world with no wars. She has heard him singing.

After Milka has said goodbye to the doctor and waved at Miss Maya she takes a hold of her papa's hand and holds on tighter than she has ever done. She knows she went outside to keep the dog safe; to take him with them to the border, she knows it wasn't her fault the bomb came then. So she has forgiven herself; Miss Maya was right. She understands now.

She feels the squeeze of her papa's hand and she knows it's time to go.

"Ready?" he whispers.

"Yes."

But before they leave, Milka turns around. First she reads the sign that hangs crooked on the red front door.

Then she reads Rule #1 above it: *Stay as long as you need.*
Her papa's fingers wrap over hers. Now she looks up to see
her soldier standing in the window, but he doesn't look at
her; she is looking skyward. It makes her think about the
English scientist but no one has seen him since the day the
apple fell on his head. So she thinks whatever it was he was
thinking about – he must've figured it out.

The Wedding Next Door

Gill James

"Mama asked me to give you this." The boy from next door was holding out a stiff envelope.

Dotty looked into his dark brown eyes. They were really serious today. His eyebrows were raised as if asking a question.

"What is it?"

"You will have to open it and see, Mrs Fellows," said the boy.

Dotty slid the card out of its envelope. It was so colourful it made her eyes smart. There was a picture of a young Pakistani girl dressed in a very elaborate dress. There was a lot of yellow in it. The girl had reddish brown patterns all over her hands and arms. The strange squiggles on the card meant nothing to Dotty. There were obviously some letters printed there but she couldn't make out what they were, let alone what any of the words might mean. "So, what's this then?"

"It's an invitation to my sister's wedding. Mama wants you to come." He bit his lip and looked away from her slightly. "You will come, won't you? Mama is worried that it might be noisy. There will be drums."

"When is it?"

"Saturday. This Saturday."

"I don't know. I think I've got something else on." Perhaps she could go and see her daughter. Get away from the noise that way.

"Please come. We'd like you to be there." He waved and scampered back up the garden path.

He wasn't a bad lad. He had a strange name, though. Majid. Like 'magic' but with a d at the end. At least he could speak English. His grandmother only spoke Urdu. His mother tried her best, but she spoke so fast and with such a heavy accent that Dotty couldn't understand her. The two girls were so shy that they never talked to anyone. Which one was getting married, she wondered? The tall thin girl. Or the shorter one who wore glasses? She had no idea which one was older. She supposed it was an arranged marriage. That's what they did, didn't they?

Majid always spoke beautifully. Perhaps it was because he went to that posh school. She's seen him walking past her house in his uniform. Her daughter had gone to the girls' equivalent and done very well. The boy's school had more status though. Majid seemed to get on well with the other boys. There was a constant stream of nicely-spoken white boys going to the house.

Dotty took the invitation in and propped it on the mantelshelf. Drums, eh? Whatever next?

Well, at least she'd got used to the cooking smells. In fact she'd even found lately that after just a few minutes she didn't notice the smell at all. It had been terrible that first week though. It had been twice a day as well. On the Wednesday her washing had been outside and she'd rushed to take it in.

They must be cooking in the garden, she thought. The smell was overpowering and it made her feel sick.

She put up with it for a week but then she just had to go round there. Her heart was beating violently as she rang the doorbell. What if they were aggressive or what if she couldn't understand?

Majid opened the door. He was about eight then. He smiled up at her and she couldn't help noticing, despite how awkward she felt, that he had the most beautiful eyes.

"Is your mummy in?" she asked.

The boy called out something she didn't understand.

She assumed it must be Urdu.

A few seconds later a young woman appeared in the doorway. She was dressed in a most peculiar fashion. She had on silky turquoise leggings and a bright pink dress in a different sort of silky material over the top. They were very pretty but didn't look suitable for the autumnal weather they were now experiencing. She also had on high-heeled shoes that looked totally impractical for housework. Perhaps most incongruous of all was the shabby grey cardigan that she wore over the tunic.

"Good morning," said Dotty. "I'm Mrs Fellows from next door. I hope you don't mind me mentioning this, but I've just had to take my washing in."

The young woman smiled. "HelloMrsFellow.I'mvery pleasedtomeetyou.IamNadiaKalparI'msorryaboutyour washinghowcanIhelp?"

Dotty frowned. Well, it sounded like English. Not quite though, and in any case she couldn't make it out. She took a deep breath. Perhaps if she spoke very slowly she could make the woman understand. It might encourage the woman to slow down herself. "You see cooking outside isn't the done thing in England. We cook in our kitchens."

The woman frowned. The she laughed. "No,no,no.We cookinthekitchentoo.Butitmustbetehspicesyou'renotusedto I'llremembertoshutthewindowifyourwashing'sout."

Dotty shook her head. "I'm sorry. I just don't understand you."

Majid then appeared in the doorway again. He said something to his mother in Urdu. She laughed.

He turned to Dotty. "My mama always talks too fast."

His mother said something else to him.

Majid turned back to Dotty. "My mother says she doesn't cook in the garden. She cooks in the kitchen like you do. But she'll try to remember to shut the kitchen window if you've got your washing's out. We use hot spices in our food. They must smell funny to you."

Dotty felt herself blush. What a fool she'd made of herself. The young woman was smiling at her. Dotty turned again to Majid. "What's your mummy's name?"

"Nadia Kalpar and I'm Majid."

"I'm Dotty Fellows."

Well, after that, she frequently heard next door's kitchen window bang as she put out her washing or went into the garden for anything else. The smell carried on, though, but she got used to it. She could set her clock by it. 10.45 in the morning and 4.45 in the evening. Two full cooked meals a day. At least these women made a lot of effort.

She even missed them when they didn't happen. Like the time the ambulance turned up to take the old man to hospital. Sadly he didn't make it. She took some flowers round to the house but nobody answered the door. She left them on the step and then worried for two whole days about whether she'd done the right thing. At the end of the week though she'd seen Nadia Kalpar who'd said, "Thankyou somuchfortheflowersMrsFellows.We'regraduallyleaning yourEnglsihway.Itwassokind." The old lady had waved and smiled from the window. That, and having heard the word 'flowers' in Nadia's garbled speech assured Dotty that she hadn't done anything wrong.

She drew the line though at trying the food. Majid often popped round with a small foil-wrapped parcel. "Mama said you might like to try some nihari." Or "Mama has made too much daal. She said you might enjoy some." She'd thanked him politely and then put the package in the bin as soon as he'd gone back home.

She'd protested when they first came. Even Sarah had come to try and persuade the landlord, Mr Montgomery, not to let the house next door to 'foreigners'.

"Goodness knows what sort of diseases they'll bring with them. They'll bring their filthy habits with them as well. Don't they overcrowd, anyway?"

"It's a big house next door. It's got attic space which your mum hasn't. There are two more bedrooms up there, so they've got five in total. It won't be overcrowded. There's the couple and her parents and three children. All the kids can have their own bedroom."

"It'll pull down the tone of the area, though. They might be all right. But some of the others who move in won't be. Can't you let the house to an English family?"

Mr Montgomery shrugged and shook his head. "Not many white people want to rent these houses. They buy their own or manage to get one from the council. Besides, these Pakistani families are much better than the white people at paying their rent. They're a nice family. Really they are."

Dotty put her hand in front of her mouth. She'd always paid on time, hadn't she? She and Albert had always had the money ready every Saturday morning at eleven o'clock sharp. They'd kept the book and the cash in the old china cottage-shaped jam dish. Not that Mr Montgomery called round any more. These days the rent went straight from her bank account into his. Her pension came in the day before. All very convenient really.

"Oh I don't mean you, Mrs Fellows. You've always been a perfect tenant."

There was no persuading him.

"You ought to think about coming and living with me and David," said Sarah after he'd gone. "You can help me with Claire."

Dotty shook her head. "No, I prefer to keep myself to myself. I think we'll just have to see what happens." She didn't like David one little bit. She was fairly certain he was having an affair. He was often late home from work and was always making excuses to go out at the weekend, leaving Sarah and Claire at home. As for Claire – they'd thoroughly spoilt that child and she was constantly badly behaved.

She would just put up with the new neighbours. They couldn't be that bad could they? She could always draw her curtains and lock her doors at night.

Her own fears of course had been encouraged by those visits she used to make with Aunt Ella to Handsworth market. There were only a few immigrants in those days and they seemed very strange indeed: tall, thin women dressed either in long dresses that seemed to just be wrapped around them or in leggings with a dress over the top. Always very silky and always very brightly coloured.

Aunt Ella would wrinkle up her nose. "They stink. It's garlic, you know. They use it in everything." Aunt Ella was a greengrocer but she refused to stock garlic even for her new neighbours. "You know, they come in asking for it but I tell them I'm not going to get it in for them. It might spoil the food for my regulars."

Poor Aunt Ella. She did manage to keep the shop going until about a year before she died but it only just about covered the cups of tea and cake she gave to her regulars. If only she'd stocked garlic and peppers and a few spices she would have made a fortune.

She used to wrestle with the Asian women at the market as she and they rummaged through the remnant box. "Do you see that? She snatched that right out of my hand."

Dotty thought she was mistaken though. These women were only interested in the sparkly pieces of material while Aunt Ella went for the florals and tweeds.

Aunt Ella would snort. "They come here and don't

bother to learn our language. This used to be a respectable little town."

Dotty had to give her that. It was disconcerting to hear them jabbering away in words you didn't understand. You always thought they were talking about you.

Yes definitely: some of her fear she felt when the Kalpars first moved in had been planted there by Aunt Ella. She'd felt really depressed when she'd seen the two women and the two girls with their hair covered and wearing silky dresses and leggings.

Oh dear. She glanced at the invitation on the mantelpiece. What should she do about this wedding? It would be rude not to go. She dreaded it though. All that noise and fuss. She hadn't got anything to wear and even if she had it would probably be too English and it wouldn't look right. Then she wouldn't be able to eat the food and they'd probably work out that she'd never even tried some of the things they'd given her.

She would just have to ring Sarah and see if she could spend the day with them. She went to the phone and pressed the speed-dial number for her daughter. Sarah picked up almost immediately.

"Hi Mum. I'm a bit busy at the moment…"

"I'll be quick. Is there any chance I can come and see you on Saturday? Only they're having a big wedding next door. I don't want to offend them by not going but I don't think I can put up with it."

"That's the thing, though, Mum. David's taking me away for a romantic weekend."

Interesting. Was this a guilt trip?

"Well what about Claire? Surely you're not taking her? Do you want me to come and look after her?"

"We're paying her friend's mum to look after her. It would have saved us a packet if you'd suggested this earlier." Sarah sighed. "I've got to go now. I'm going clothes shopping. Got to make the effort for David, haven't I? You'd better pretend you're ill."

The phone went dead.

Oh well, she supposed she'd better go. Could she say she was ill when she wasn't? Probably not. She wasn't very good at lying. And anyway, perhaps she'd had a lucky escape. Looking after Claire all weekend on her own might have been even more challenging than a few drums.

As it happened she didn't have to pretend. She woke up on Saturday morning with terrible indigestion. It must have been that banana she ate. It had been particularly under ripe and bananas gave her indigestion at the best of times. But her GP had said that bananas were good because of the potassium in them so she always made the effort.

Still it was the perfect excuse to get out of the wedding. She'd wrapped up a small gift for the bride; a set of teaspoons. She'd got them at the market and she didn't even know if the girl would need them. She'd heard that she would be going to live with her husband's family so they'd probably already have teaspoons there. Never mind, it was the thought that counted, surely.

She put on the suit she usually wore for church. Just after nine she made her way round to her neighbour's. Already their narrow street was filling up with cars and a gentle rhythmic drumming was coming from the back of the house.

Nadia opened the door.

"OhMrsFellows.Nicetoseeyouwon'tyoucomein?"

"I'm not staying. I don't feel too well. But I've brought your daughter a present." She thrust the small packet into Nadia's hand.

Nadia frowned and then smiled. "Mostkind,MrsFellows. Ihopeyoufeelbettersoon.I'llsendMajidroundwithsomesomosas later."

Dotty nodded and made her way back to her own house. She sank down on the sofa and closed her eyes. She dozed for a while.

When she woke up a while later the indigestion was worse and the drumming was louder. Her heart seemed to be beating in time to the drums. It was thumping up into her rib cage. There was another noise as well. What was it? There it was again. Of course. The doorbell.

She went to get up off the sofa but as she did the pain in her chest intensified and she couldn't catch her breath.

The doorbell rang again.

"Coming!" she shouted. She couldn't move though and she couldn't help crying out. Would this pain please stop? She'd never had indigestion this bad before.

"Mrs Fellows. Are you all right? I've bought you some samosas."

"Pain..." Dotty managed to say. She didn't know whether she'd said it loud enough. The pain kicked in again. She screamed.

"Mrs Fellows, don't worry. I'll get some help."

Dotty couldn't quite work out what happened next but suddenly Majid and Nadia were there and a tall good-looking young man she had never seen before. Nadia was holding her hand.

"We'vesentforanambulance.Don'tworrymynewsoninlaw isadoctor."

"The ambulance is on its way. You're having a heart attack," said the young man. "The paramedics will be able to stabilise you. They'll be here very soon. Just keep calm and breathe through the pain."

"My sister's fiancé is training to be a doctor," said Majid.

They were kind at the hospital. Within a couple of days Dotty was feeling back to normal. The only problem was the food; it was atrocious.

"They won't let you out unless you start eating properly. Or unless you agree to come and live with us," Sarah nagged.

"It's pigswill. I can't eat that." She was really hungry now but the food was always greasy and cold and any meat was always too tough to chew. She was frightened it would give her indigestion and she would think she was having another heart attack.

"Well, think about it, Mum. You're putting a strain on the NHS at the moment. I've got to go now. David will be expecting his dinner. It's costing me a fortune, driving backwards and forwards to the hospital. And the parking. Never mind as well all the time it takes."

Oh dear. She would have to make an effort. She really didn't want to go to her daughter's.

"She's gone?" said the young nurse who was Dotty's particular favourite.

Dotty nodded.

"Good. Then I can let your other visitors in. I think they're much more eager to spend time with you."

Dotty looked up to see Nadia and Majid walking towards her. Majid was grinning and Nadia was carrying a large packet wrapped in tinfoil.

"So nice to see you," said Dotty.

"Wevebroughtyousomesamosasasyoudidn'tgettoeaet anyattheweddding.Theyr'efresh."

"I helped make them," said Majid. He took the packet off his mother and started opening it.

Oh, it looked as if she was really going to have to try some of their food this time. Perhaps she could distract them. "Do you have any photos of the wedding?"

Nadia beamed. She took out her phone and showed Dotty. Goodness, the girl did look pretty despite the glasses. There was that handsome young man as well who had come to her rescue. "Shelovedtheteapsonsnandwillwritetosaythank yousoon."

Majid was twitching the packet restlessly. "Don't you want to try one of my samosas, Mrs Fellows?"

"Just one other thing first. How did you manage to get in so easily when I was taken ill?"

"OhMrMontomeryaskedustokeepakeyjsutincase."

Dotty frowned. That young woman really must learn to slow down.

"The landlord gave us a key to your house and asked us to keep an eye on you, Mrs Fellows." Majid was now holding the samosas right in front of Dotty's nose. She couldn't help but notice how good they smelled.

"Well, I think I'll have to have words with that Mr Montgomery."

"Please, Mrs Fellows, try one of my samosas." Majid was getting quite stressed now.

Without stopping to think Dotty took a samosa and bit into it. Crisp pastry and beautifully cooked vegetables with just a hint of spice melted into her mouth. She had never tasted anything so exquisite.

Nadia and Majid stared at her as she chewed. "Do you like it, Mrs Fellows?" said Majid.

"Oh, I do."

"Would you like another?"

"Yes, please."

Dotty ate the second one greedily then had an idea. She signalled to the nurse.

"Look she said. I'm eating now and my good friends here, my next-door neighbours, are willing to keep an eye on me. Do you think I can go home soon?"

Nadia and Majid nodded enthusiastically.

The nurse laughed. "I should think so. I'll get hold of

one of the doctors and see what they say."

Dotty turned back to her visitors as she took a third samosa. "And will your other daughter be getting married soon? I'm looking forward to another wedding. With drums."

Shqiperia

Jennifer Burkinshaw

24 December 2018

This isn't the top of the world but it *is* an immense, high plateau, *radiant* with full, orange sun picking out crystals in its pristine swathes of snow. Planting myself right in the middle, I stretch my arms as wide as they'll go and revolve slowly to embrace the mountains of Albania that rise up all around me. In front of me towers a set of white, jagged teeth; the snow has slipped off the face of the one to my right, baring fawn rock. In contrast, on my left, is the snowy, curved shoulder of the mountain Maren could be on, not so far above me now.

Hugging the far edge of this sunny circle is a trio of small chalets. No sign of life at all but that no longer fools me. Only when I've actually been into each one, am I convinced that no one's been here for a long, long time.

Returning to the centre, I want to linger on its welcoming warmth and safety – you could see anybody coming from any direction. If only Maren *had* been in one of those chalets and we could glory in being together, here in his own stunning homeland.

Homeland – the word shoots an angry pain across my heart. As of twelve hours ago, the first and last time I met Maren's parents, I know he *has* no homeland anymore. First he's exploited in *my* homeland; then deported; and within *hours* of arriving home, hounded from his *own* country by a ridiculous, medieval blood-feud. And – irony of ironies – one that comes full circle: by 'absconding' from his gang masters and the deadly cockling in Morecambe Bay, he apparently 'dishonoured' the Albanian middleman who found the job.

So, if he's up here somewhere, as his brother thinks he might be, I've got to find him, before dark, before he crosses the mountains into Kosovo and disappears forever.

I retrace my steps to the path, eyes down to position my sodden trainers in my own knee-deep footprints.

When I glance up, I stop dead in my tracks. A dark figure. Stalking steadily towards me. Wielding a rifle. And it's pointed at me.

It's Madman, the recluse from lower down the mountain! Having brandished his hunting knife at me a couple of hours ago, stolen my food, he's come to gun me down for daring to continue up 'his' mountain!

Sweat breaks out all over my body and I'm sharply nauseous. Is this stunning plateau the place I'm going to die, these dramatic mountains the only witnesses?

But this person isn't bearded like Madman, nor as old. Has Maren's 'avenger' followed me after all?

I don't know the range of a shotgun but I'm not going to make it any easier for its owner: heart drumming in my ears, I sit down.

He's advancing slowly, so slowly, towards me, the gun barrel to his cheek. Time's also in slow motion; my every sense sharpens; I inhale deeply of the pure, sun-warmed air and it steadies my breathing. Gazing up in wonder at the beauty of the circle of mountains, at my mountain, I wonder if Maren was up there after all; whether he'll hear the shot and he be the one to find me. That's some small comfort.

The gunman's near enough for me to hear his footsteps shooshing through the melting snow. I want to say a prayer but words won't come. So I just *think*. Over and over I think, *Let me live*. Eighteen years on this earth is not enough; not anywhere *near* enough. I can't *not* see again my friends, my parents, my grandmother. And Maren, the

119

reason I'm here. Does this *prove* we were a bad idea? My brain can't think clearly enough.

I scrunch my eyes closed.

Now I hear the rustling of his clothes. How close do you have to *be* to shoot someone?

"Tess?" he says.

I scrabble to my feet. Is he there? Behind that coppery stubble?

It's the same bottle green padded coat he was wearing by Morecambe Bay two months ago when he came back to find me.

Maren. My Maren.

My body needs to sink against him but he's still holding the gun, now across his chest, as stunned as I am, and even more flabbergasted.

"Why are you here, Tess? Is it my family?"

The green of his eyes is heavy with fear.

"No, no, not them. They're fine. I saw them last night."

His shoulders sag in relief; he closes his eyes.

Then they flash open in alarm. "But then you could have led the enemy to me."

My eyes flood. I've made a huge mistake in coming.

"How *did* you find me – I mean *after* you had somehow found my house? I told *no* one where I was going."

My mouth's so distorted, I can only heave out a few words between sobs.

"Your parents said… I must leave today… for Tiran… the airport. But I was looking… at photos in your room. Then… Kade came and… he saw one of you… with him and your mum… in these mountains. *He* said… maybe you were here; he *said* you'd *want* to see me."

I finish in a rush, just before I'm en*gulfed* by floods of tears that are formed from exhaustion, hunger but, most of all, sheer devastation. He *doesn't* want to see me! And I *could* have endangered him – for nothing.

He says nothing. When I finally look up at him, he's staring beyond my shoulder at the way up here, lost in thoughts I can't fathom. I don't know you, I think. This has all been a monumental mistake and I'm going to have to go home, which doesn't feel like home any more. I *thought* home was where you were.

Instead I tell him, "Kade brought me to the foot of the mountain in the dark. No one knew. Not even your parents. We cycled all the way here. We were *so* careful."

Now he looks at me. For the first time at me, maybe now believing he could be safe after all. He licks his lips and his face softens.

"You need to rest," he says.

And to eat, I think – I'm *shaky* weak with hunger now.

He slings the rifle over his shoulder by its strap and leads the way back to the track.

Back at the fork in the road, where I took the one that led me to him, Maren takes the darker one, up into a wood. Pine trees, stretch out friendly, snow-clad arms on either side of us but they allow the sun in only in stripes so I soon become shivery; and the ever steeper path is draining the dregs of my energy.

Up and
up and
up.

Maren keeps glancing behind – to check we're not being followed or impatience with me? In a bone-weary stupor, all I can do is put one foot in front of the other, my eyes fixed on the ground, where thick tree roots poke through the snow, trying to trip me.

Somehow, I've caught up with him. Because he's stopped!

"This is…" He looks past me, down the path we've just climbed.

A dilapidated chalet, its wood almost black with age, is tucked into a dark corner of the forest.

Maren strides across a wooden veranda, logs stacked neatly all the way along the wall on either side of the door. I follow him in.

He stands his gun by the door.

An ancient looking bed and a wooden table with two attached benches are crowded in the half to my left. In fact, that's all the furniture there is.

"I had to move everything near the fire," he says, following the direction of my gaze. "This place, I do not know the owner. I just borrow, for… a few nights. On my way."

My heart grips. When does he leave? I daren't ask – I haven't got it in me to go back down this mountain today; to set off to Tirana alone.

I join him at the small window opposite the door.

There it is! My plateau, that brought me Maren, no longer orange but rosy in the dying sun.

"So beautiful," I whisper, sucking in a breath.

"I pick this place so I can see someone coming."

He nods at the other window which looks out down the forest path we've just climbed.

I bite my lip to hold back the tears, humiliated by my naivety in thinking there was still room for beauty in his life, but more at the danger he feels himself in. Which *I* could have now added to. I hoped once we'd come inside, he'd hold me; *I'd* hold *him*. But now it's obvious – he blames me for his deportation. It *should* have been safe: he'd not come back to Morecambe Bay to find me until his gang masters were inside – *I'd* identified them, secured their conviction; but apparently his Albanian contact had been surveilling me all along; phoned the police, shopped him.

Wrecked in every sense, I have to sit on the bed.

"You need to eat," he tells me.

Crouching, he criss-crosses some logs in the hearth and puts a match to them.

"Aren't you worried the smoke will give you away?"

"The trees are very tall all around, and anyway," he shrugs, "we have to live."

My heart clings on to that 'we', even as my head reminds me it's only until he can get rid of me.

"Can you wait until this is hot?" he asks, holding up a battered pan.

I shake my head. He empties it onto a tin plate on the table.

I sit at the bench nearest the fire. Meat. No idea whose. I wait for my veggie stomach to recoil. It doesn't! I grab the knife and fork and demolish the lot till there's only a heap of small bones left.

Maren's blowing on the fire, fanning it into life. He smiles faintly when he sees I've finished already.

"Sleep now," he tells me. "I go to get dinner."

Maybe sharing my image of some takeaway up here, he almost smiles again. Almost.

As he picks up his rifle again, I push off my trainers.

Once the door's closed, I peel off my jeans and put them to dry by the fire. I wriggle down into Maren's sleeping bag. It smells of him, of course but instead of a delicious comfort, now he only wants rid of me, it's a bitter rebuke. Me coming here was at least as big a mistake as *him* coming to find me.

Better we'd *both* left it as it was when we kissed goodbye fourteen months ago, when there was only love between us. There's only so much reality a young relationship can take, I now realise sadly.

Beyond tired, I gaze into the amber flames, as if they could obliterate all the problems hanging over us.

The flames are embers when I wake, the rest of the room in complete darkness, the windows black. Cold swirls around me from behind – it's the opening of the door which has woken me. I whip round.

"It is snowing much outside," Maren says.

"Heavily," I correct as I used to do. "You think we are safe, then, once our tracks are covered?"

"I hope."

He puts something down on the hearth and piles logs onto the dying fire. I can just make out him pulling a metal stand of sorts over the new flare. On it he stands a much larger pan than before.

Then he sits on the edge of the bed. I sit up, curling my legs round to make room for him.

"Dinner," he tells me.

I try to smile but it hurts too much, this... detached civility with *me*. He's only used my name once, for heaven's sake – when he first saw me – as if it's something he can't bear to have in his mouth. When I so love how it sounds on his lips.

I take a deep breath. "Maren, you came to find me; the next minute it happens, the very thing you'd spent sixteen months avoiding. I didn't know I was being watched and even if I had, I had no way of telling you. But it feels like you blame me."

He shakes his head. "No. *I* chose to come. It was a mistake I must live with. But *we* cannot be any more. You must see that," he urges. "I can *never* come to England again. Now I cannot even stay in Albania. How do you think you can *ever* see me when I must always move?"

When I still don't speak he looks at me in the gloaming. God! That look takes me back to the very first time we met,

124

when there was already regret in his mouth. Should we never have got started? Were we *always* impossible? I begin to understand – it's not that he doesn't, or couldn't care, it's just that some things really *can* stop love.

"You mean?" I ask him, "We always *were* a bad idea?"

He smiles wryly at me. I used that exact phrase on him the night I discovered he was an illegal cockler.

"We have made a lot of… trouble between us," he says, rueful now. "But even now I would not call us 'a bad idea', Tess."

I give a tearful laugh. I'm not sure whether he's just trying to make me feel a bit better, but it's a… gracious thing to say. The atmosphere is clearer, lighter between us.

Settling back against the opposite bed head, he swings his legs up.

I take another deep breath. "What was it like, Maren, in the detention centre?"

He shakes his head. "Thankfully – short."

He won't let me in, then. I understand why – he's had and will have to be, self-reliant and tough. *And* he's proud and pragmatic – talking about it, churning back through it, changes nothing, he'll believe.

Instead I tell him about my flight to Tirana, the fog, delay, being ripped off by a woman who gave me a lift.

As I get to the part about his home town, he leans forward, drinking in every word.

"You spoke to no one?"

I shake my head. His family was also terrified an English girl in town would draw attention to herself, to *them*, suggesting Maren was around to his avenger.

"And people ask why I want to leave Albania!" he rants. "These ridiculous blood feuds. It is from the time of the castles, truly. There are over a thousand rules – the kanun, which is over 500 years old!"

"What sort of rules?" I ask, mystified.

He scoffs. "Crazy things, like a man's life is the same whether he is handsome or ugly; or… the murderer can only move around at night; and he may not fire his gun at women, children, livestock or house, only at men."

Crazy they might be, but this 'code' also makes this threat to Maren all too… precise and possible. The fine down at my hair line stirs.

And all this because he 'dared' to leave behind a job that nearly took his life. If I hadn't been there watching for him as he was out on the Sands at night, he'd have drowned in quicksand.

"Banning hakmari was the one good thing under communism," he says. "After liberation, it grew strong again. Now many even ask for asylum because of it."

"Do they get it?" I see a sudden hope.

"Hardly ever. And remember, I am never permitted to go back to the UK. Instead, in my own country, I am a dead man walking."

I shudder at the phrase. No wonder he greeted me with a rifle instead of open arms!

"Your brother sent you a message," I tell him, as a distraction.

He looks up.

"Gezuar Krishtlindjet!"

I'm worried as I say it – now's the second year he's been away from his family at Christmas, and for how many more to come? But his eyes light up.

"It's Christmas Eve, Tess! When you have come all this way, it would be rude not to invite you for Christmas!"

A thrill runs through my stomach at his great gift for living in the now; that he can be excited at Christmas just with me, in this basic cabin!

"It would rude for me not to accept your invitation," I

tell him, grinning. "What do you do in Albania on Christmas Eve?"

"A great feast…" he trails off, looking regretfully at the one pan.

"Have you looked on the shelves?"

"I do not want to steal their stuff."

"We could leave them some of my lek?"

A couple of minutes later, he's back with an old oil lamp and some tins.

He shares my smile. Something feels… settled between us. And we have a bit of time.

26 December

"Oh no," I tell him, glancing from the old-fashioned wooden sledge to the near vertical hillside in front of us.

"It is a *fast* way to get the plateau you love," he says, gazing down on it, spot lit again by the midday sun.

Still I shake my head.

"Look at it, Tess – no trees, nothing in the way, no fence or wall at the bottom. What is the worst thing to happen?"

"We both break our necks and die."

"No, the worst thing, my feet are brakes."

He holds out his hand to me. My heart's hammering out of my chest, I glance between the gleaming, virgin snow and his face, for once facing fun instead of the threats of unscrupulous men. I take his hand.

Horizontal to the… precipice, we get ourselves good and settled. His arms are tight round mine and I lean back right into him, gluing us together.

"Hey! Your heart's pounding as much as mine."

His cheek grazes mine. "Yes, fear but do it anyway. It will be."

Sentence hanging, he pushes us over the edge.

No turning; hurtling only down, icy air whipping past us,

127

gathering speed. Mountains, plateau, untouched snow all in fast motion. I'm shrieking. Faster, ever faster. Till Maren's yelling too, in my ear. Terrifying; thrilling; exhilarating.

But how will it end?

Maren tries to drop his feet from the rails to slow us down – can't be done, waay too fast.

"Ditch ahead!" I scream over my shoulder.

He pulls me off sideways; winded, I topple away from him downhill, over and over till a snow drift catches me. Coughing out ice, I scrabble up, peering around for him.

"Maren!" I yell, scrambling down, thigh-deep in snow.

I told him we'd break our necks. Oh God, he could be dead even. What a stupid way to die! I'll kill him!

I slide to my knees next to where he's lying face up, eyes closed.

"Maren," I breathe, putting my hand on his cheek. "Please be all right."

I'm trying to remember all the stuff you're told about not moving people. Madman – I'll have to go for him. But he won't have a clue what I'm saying. And anyway, by the time I've got there, it'll be too late.

A green eye appears. Then another.

"Maren! Can you see me? Are you hurt?"

"Awesome!"

It takes me a moment to realise that instead of answering my questions, he's finishing the sentence he started at the top.

"*I'll* hurt you!" I thump on his chest with my fists.

"Hey!" he says, grabbing my wrists to stop me. "What is that for?"

"You know what! Don't ever take me on a ride like that again!"

"You sure, Tess?" he says, still gripping my wrists. "Do you not feel… alive?"

I sit back on heels and look down at my plateau not so far below us now. And he's right. I've never felt more alive than on this mountain of ours, under the sun, with *him*.

"Of course," I tell him, as he sits up.

His smile crinkles his eyes.

We tramp down the rest of the hill first to retrieve the sledge, which is end-on in the ditch, then to the plateau.

Maren sits on the sledge, then tips back to gaze into the cloudless sky.

"I love your country, Maren," I tell him. "Thank you, Shqiperia!" I tell all the mountains surrounding us, their unique shapes white against the blue.

He smiles happily, still on the sledge.

"Look!"

Two massive brown birds are wheeling above us, with all the space and freedom the world has to offer. No borders and visas for them. No justifying why you're in different airspace. No categories or hierarchies. Birds build nests, but belong *no*where.

"Eagles. Gold eagles. Here, Tess."

He shifts off the sledge so I don't have to keep craning my neck.

For so long they soar over the plateau, as if just enjoying it as much as we are, though maybe they're looking for food.

Gradually, their range decreases till end they end up circling each other, getting closer and closer. Then they actually lock talons! Their wings fold half way in and they start to cascade chaotically through the sky, like us tumbling down the sledging field!

"God, Maren! What are they playing at? Fighting?"

"No, the opposite. Er…" To the side of me, his hand whirrs as he searches for the word.

"Mating? They're *mating?!*"

"No, not that. Not yet. That cannot happen in the air. This is *before* they mate."

"Courting? So that's it! But they'll end up dead if they don't spread their wings again!"

They're in freefall!

As if they've heard me, they pull apart and turn out, like from a vertical dance floor they're now returning to the top of. Then they start the whole whirl again.

"When will they have enough of courting?" I sit up to look at Maren.

"When they both feel ready for... making love. Then they mate for life."

His shyness, his choosing of the *right* phrase, sends the heat of a blush down my face. We were once so close to it but I know he believes it's so *binding*, it's not for those who can't be together. Not for us.

"Do you think that's where they've gone?"

The pair's shrunk into the distance before disappearing over the toothy mountain.

"Maybe," he smiles.

He comes to straddle the sledge, facing me.

"We were lucky to see this. You know, Shqiperia, it means Land of the Eagles?"

"Ah – that's why the symbol on your passports."

"Looking opposite ways – one north and one south."

"But why eagles?"

"It is a story... a myth. A hunter, in the mountains, maybe here, saved a baby eagle from a snake. To thank him, the parent eagle gave him good, clear eyesight and the power of its wings for his arms. So he could hunt better but also fight off the enemy.

The eagle also gave him the name which means 'son of the eagle', Shqipetar."

"And so Shqiperia," I murmur, looking into his eyes.

"And Shqipetar, maybe that's you – strong enough to feed yourself *and* banish the enemy."

"I hope," he says, shortly.

I shiver: the sun's just sunk behind face-slip mountain; we've had the best of today. And dark clouds have begun to gather overhead.

"Time to go," Maren says.

He stands and reaches for my hands to pull me with him.

We're quiet as we leave the now gloomy plateau – tired, hungry, but, most of all, desolate.

Desolate that we're not eagles. Tomorrow we must part forever: me back to the country which banished him; him to he-doesn't-know-where, from a country that first could offer him no prospect of a job and now hounds him from it with a brutal, barbaric blood-feud. Countries that have lost their way.

Perfect Day

Matevž Hönn

Britte awakens at 7:15 (GMT +2:00). She has slept better than usual; her husband, Klaus, set off on a business trip, last evening. She doesn't know that during the night, Ms. Xhebe, a woman from Sierra Leone, was run over by a truck on the highway connecting Freetown to the port from which a ferry can be taken to the Lungi International Airport. Likewise, she has no idea that while she takes a morning piss, the mob in the suburbs of Mexico City is cutting Juanito's left leg with a rusting hacksaw because his results were not good, recently. In order to increase the average daily turnover more for the little beggar (originally from El Arenal, Hidalgo Municipality), the mob is considering amputating both of his legs, but the recent study from Berkeley University shows that the average transportation costs for the beggar rise 6.5% in such a case, and the butchering might not be feasible. Britte doesn't pay attention to the color of her urine, and there is no need to. Her doctor told her to be afraid of cerebral hemorrhage, as it runs in her family. Her pussy and ass will be in good condition even a day or two after her death. There is mist hanging over Stuttgart, and Klaus will call soon. Britte doesn't know that her husband is banging whores on business trips; neither is she familiar with statistics of sex tourism involving Germans; neither did she subscribe for the data from UNICEF alarming honest people that many millions of children in China don't have access to proper education and thus many girls end up in prostitution rings.

Southwest of Stuttgart on the West Bank, 35-year-old Nazeera is looking for her youngest son: "Masud! Masud!

I will break your spine if you don't come home immediately. I'll smash it with grandfather's olive branch, Masud! You won't leave the house again!"

Britte prepares coffee with little sugar. She doesn't know that a gypsy woman in Romania is charging €70 for reading futures from the cup. Britte earns €5,393 per month for whatever job she does. She switches on her mobile. Klaus will phone in 2 minutes. She is not worried about his safety. After all, Lufthansa spends a good portion of government support improving textbooks and manuals for the pilots.

"Hallo."
"Hallo."
"Good flight?"
"Slept like a baby. You?"
"Never better."
"Call you later."
"Sure. Tschüss."
"Tschüss."

The above dialogue runs like a Mercedes E-Class Coupe. If you are careful enough, you can use it for 30 years without particular maintenance. If Britte possessed a bit of my sense of humor, she would reply to Klaus, "Of course you slept like a baby, you fat pig; I wonder how did the others in the cabin sleep, listening to that snoring and farting of yours? You are lucky you didn't bring the whole goddamn airbus down in the Mongolian desert." Unfortunately for their marriage and for her social circle, she is a completely humorless woman. Neither Klaus nor Britte is aware that during their ritual exchange of nastiness, 7,600 km away in Jacksonville (Florida), Raul Packmanchampion chooses a Kalashnikov AK 47, produced in Romania, from a remarkable collection in a 24-hour gun store. It's a hell of a gun, and Raul is of legal age.

Britte buys vegetables at Hasan's kiosk. She read an article in *Der Spiegel* about Albanian mafia controlling the drug trade and prostitution all over Europe, but not her Hasan. He is so nice and speaks German perfectly.

"Guten Tag, Frau Strossmayer."

"Servus, Hasan. Nice cabbage you have here."

Depending on the season, the reader is free to replace 'cabbage' with other vegetables.

"Fresh from Macedonia."

"…and carrots."

"Got them in the morning. 2.5 €/kg."

Another Mercedes Coupe for 30 years. Though assembled by immigrants, the quality control system is kept at a high level by German engineers. In order to keep the dialogue up to date, the demanding reader should raise the prices of vegetables for a yearly inflation index of 3.5% in post-war Germany. After all, even a Mercedes needs oil from time to time. Hasan passes the recyclable bag with vegetables to Britte. She doesn't pay attention to his hairy hands with a huge golden ring on his middle finger. Hasan's ring is in the shape of a horseshoe and a size or two bigger than necessary. Should the Nationalsozialistische Deutsche Arbeiterpartei win an election and open the concentration camps again, it wouldn't need to chop off his finger in order to collect the ring.

I bet it is 18:30 in North Korea already. Comrade Pak Jin Fu sits at his work table in the secured room near the kitchen. He works as a food taster in the presidential bunker in Pyongyang. If an atomic bomb exploded above him, he would feel it merely like a distant fart.

At about the same time, I descend the steps leading to the outdoor recreational facilities at InterContinental Eros Hotel in Delhi. Thank God for the knee system with the thigh bone, tibia, and kneecap, stabilized by the ligaments and lateral and medial meniscus serving as shock absorbers, which enables me to descend the steps smoothly. Work of art, really! Without it, I would descend the steps like a dead dolphin.

The white rhinoceros population in the West Bank is zero. Masud hides behind the garbage container a few yards from the Israeli checkpoint. In his pockets, he feels four round rocks he collected earlier near the West Bank of the river Jordan. The stones are not pieces of fossiliferous upper-cretaceous limestone, predominant in Palestine, but reddish Nubian sandstone of which the tombs of Petra are carved. These rocks were formatted from the cambrian or cretaceous periods and would, Masud hopes, trash the helmet and deliver substantial damage to the Israeli skull if hit with the right force and at a correct angle.

For a starter, comrade Pak Jin Fu is served beef carpaccio with marinated bean salad. "He...he! My lucky day! Argentinean beef! Argentineans better keep an eye on their generals in order to prevent history from repeating. No...they wouldn't try to assassinate our dear president."

Britte walks down the Königstrasse, her hair almost shining in the almost-sunny early afternoon. Even if she knew that the female body was lying in the pit in Sierra Leone, she wouldn't know what to do with it.

And here we go. After 3,000 years of global warming transformed Germany into a desert, David Attenborough Jr. in khaki shorts and a safari hat is crawling over heated rocks. Catching his breath, he holds a small stone toward the BBC camera.

"No...no...it's not a stone. It is a small part of the fibula of a middle-aged female who habituated around here..." David inhales deeply to make an impact on the audience "3,000 years ago! She was 1.72 m tall, well built, with a brain size of 1.4 cubic centimeters, exercised moderately,

135

consumed less meat and beer than average at that time, and she voted for Angela Merkel twice."

Comrade Pak Jin Fu is served Norwegian salmon with mango salsa while his wife of 35 kg survives with a half cup of rice per day. "My lucky day! Norwegians wouldn't bother to kill our president. They are busy enough killing whales and clubbing sea lions."

It's almost dawn in Florida. Red-eyed Raul Packmanchampion rides his seventeenth-hand Ford Mustang in the direction of his college, interchangeably caressing his balls and his gun in his lap, hoping that he will arrive before classes start. He is a chain smoker of fake Marlboro. Lung cancer is far away, further than Pyongyang.

As the mob in Mexico City toasts with tequila the new business plan for beggars freshly approved by Don Domingo Sanchez, I jump in the outdoor swimming pool in the InterContinental Eros Hotel in Delhi. Above me, a bunch of crows is circling. They must have noticed that I am a bad swimmer, hoping for a bite of my ass if I drown down here. In the corner of the swimming pool, an overweight Englishman with greasy hair combed in waves (a poor imitation of the Clark Gable hairstyle from the 30s) floats in something that looks like a truck tire as he barks orders to the waiter. He completely missed the news broadcasted in most of the media; fifty years ago, the British Empire was reduced to a patch of unfertile land around London.

Masud didn't throw even one rock in the direction of the Israeli soldiers when suddenly the hell broke loose. He heard his friends shouting and saw them running away for a second before tear gas burned his eyes and lungs, causing him to vomit. The next thing he felt was being shoved to the four-billion-years-old ground. Except Hasan, none of the characters in this story would offer much resistance in situation like this. Neither would I, let alone Britte. Though her nostrils were partly numb due to years of abuse from Klaus's farts, she can't even imagine something as horrific as tear gas being pumped in her breathing system.

Morning pressure in Jacksonville is 1.010 mbar, and visibility is 7 miles. From a safe distance, Raul Packmanchampion is contemplating a schoolyard full of students like Napoleon, hidden behind the bush formerly used to observe Mikhail Kutuzov's army marching on Borodino field. Firmly gripping his Kalashnikov, he used the same word that Bonaparte used, only translated from medieval French into American English: "Motherfuckers!"

Britte is in a supermarket, and her wristwatch by Longines, the Dolce Vita series, shows 13:46:53. It is inaccurate only by 17 seconds. She is cruising toward the cashier with strong air freshener spray in an otherwise-empty basket. If I were the clerk, I would have noticed that her hands are a bit worn out, though rich moisturizers and other necessary cosmetics are applied regularly. Her fingers are not meaty; one can easily locate the precise position and shape of metacarpophalangeal joints and rounded, cut fingernails that are white and polished. But please, even the slightest hint of aggressiveness is missing. It is obvious that she doesn't use them for climbing trees or tearing apart buffalo meat, let alone seducing potentially wealthy businessmen in the nightclubs.

A glass of wine is served in the bunker in North Korea. Pak Jin Fu tastes 2005 Romanee Conti, Domaine De La Tache. "Thanks to the Workers' party for this! French secret service

137

wouldn't target our president. Their first lady smiles so sweetly; no, she wouldn't let her husband poison the wine."

Jacksonville, 7:47 EDT. Police cars and ambulances flock like wasps toward the schoolyard from different directions. George Alwayslateforclasses walks up to where Raul Packmanchampion is standing with the still-smoking gun and quickly evaluates the damage: "Shit, man." Crows detect correctly that my strokes are slower now, and they decide to descend their circling to about the 7th floor of the Eros Hotel.

Britte is having her afternoon coffee in the Schwabishe Trap Café while Juanito is dropped on the main square, Zocalo, in Mexico City. Comrade Pak Jin Fu would detect that the coffee is not flavorful Ethiopian Arabica but a cheaper Brazilian blend of beans that is 25% Arabica and 75% Robusta and thus of rather bitter taste. Though she doesn't sip too much sugar in the mug, Britte can't taste anything. If she would pay attention to the radio news aired in the coffee shop, she would hear that a couple of minutes ago, 15 students were shot dead in a college in Jacksonville. Coffee cost her €2.5, twice as much as women in Sierra Leone earn per day for cleaning rocks from the highway. Britte punches Klaus's number in her cell phone, preparing to start the goodnight Mercedes, but Klaus doesn't answer. Ms. Xhebe doesn't know Klaus, but if she had access to Google Earth in that pit of hers, she could see him fuelled by Viagra entering the Hilton Hotel in Shanghai with a Chinese escort lady. The waiter drops a customer satisfaction questionnaire on Britte's table and Britte fills it accordingly.

Jolanda Fatassbookworm is shot in the ass. If she had an ass made of the same material as a rhinoceros', she wouldn't even feel it. Unfortunately, it isn't made of the same material, and her ass will have to be amputated. Fortunately for Juanito's ass, on the other hand, the Mexican mob doesn't watch U.S. TV stations regularly!! Juanito didn't have too much luck in his life, but this time, he can't complain.

If there were bells in Pyongyang, they would beat 20:00 (GMT+9:00). For dessert, tiramisu with kahlua is served in the presidential basement. "My lucky, lucky day! The Italian prime minister is more focused on chasing women's asses than on changing the world order. What a day! No burgers, no fish and chips, no goddamn sushi from Japan! No Chinese or Russian food. The latter pretend that they are friendly, but you never know with countries with histories like theirs!" Relaxed, Pak Jin Fu lifts the wine glass and makes a toast gesture toward the armed guard at the door.

Britte rings her daughter, Sonia, who studies in Munich.
    "Father is in China. I took a day off."
    "Good for you."
    "Are you coming home for the weekend?"
    "We'll see... I have an appointment with somebody..."
    "Is that the married one?"

Sonia is a university student on the verge of adulthood; thus, their conversations don't run smoothly yet. They sound more like some alternative-energy Volkswagen prototype. In a couple of years, however, generation gaps will be filled with reliable spare parts and the course will be set for decades ahead. Sonia heard about the shooting in Jacksonville, but she knows nothing about prices for a blow job in China. If she were forced to guess, she would miss by €9.

Johnson Basketballplayer was only slightly wounded in his little finger and thus was the last one to be taken to the hospital in spite of screaming like a T-Rex and staging a bigger circus than his seriously wounded (and dead) classmates.

Mexico City's altitude is 2,240 m. Researchers from Berkeley University announced that they have ultimate proof that female tourists with silicone breast implants adjust to high altitude as quickly as tourists without them. Manuel Alfonso, owner of the farm for breeding fighting cocks, drops 5 pesos in Juanito's cap. If the boy would juggle a bit with the healthy foot or sing the Mexican national anthem, he would give him 11 pesos, but for merely lying on the street, 5 is enough. After all, Manuel received nothing for free in his life. He had to steal his first cock and then pair him with the right women in order to breed fearless fighters.

A young waiter catches Britte at the cafeteria's exit door.
    "Entschuldigen Sie bitte…"
    "Yes…" She turns around to face him.
    The demanding reader would want to know the name of the waiter. He's Dieter. "Is my German not good enough?"
    "It is fine. What are you…"
    "No…no…Is my German not good enough for you?" Dieter remarkably increases the volume. He is quite quick-tempered, for his genes were shaken a bit during the bombing of Dresden where his grandparents weathered WWII.
    "I am sorry, I…"
    "Was my service timely?" asked the waiter just when comrade Pak Jin Fu feels his stomach cramp and begins puking black blood, black as night in Pyongyang. An alarm goes off in the presidential bunker.
    "Yes…I didn't complain."

"Wasn't I polite enough?"

"Yes...I didn't..." answers Britte, trying to make sense of the situation. Sir Englishman from Delhi's swimming pool would try to solve the matter by offering a tip. The idea would not enter Britte's mind; she would, however, give a 50-cent coin to Juanito if she spotted him begging in Mexico City. Depending on my mood, I would give zero up to one dollar to the one-legged child beggar. Klaus, on the other hand, reimburses the taxi ride home for the prostitutes if he is satisfied with their services.

"So, what was wrong?" Dieter almost screams, holding the questionnaire under Britte's nose. "Didn't I bend enough?"

"Sorry...I will leave!"

"Look!" He pulls from his pocket the safety rules and regulations for waiters in Bundesrepublik Deutschland, edition 1957, and recites chapter 765: "*Waiter shouldn't bend more than 15° (upright position of the homo sapiens's spine should be taken as the base for measurement) toward customer, otherwise guest might have a feeling his private space is intruded.*"

"Excuse me, would you tell me your name, please?"

"Rudolph." Holy shit!! I had better apologize to all readers. This information was not disclosed to me before.

"I will call the manager."

"You can call me Rudi."

Britte has a feeling that this must be 'Candid Camera' or any other reality show, and her eyes circle the cafeteria for any sign that this is a joke. A UN delegation passes the body of Ms. Xhebe, riding a Hummer H3x toward the Lungi International Airport at the steady speed of 120 km/h. Each member of the delegation pushed a couple of bloody diamonds up his ass which he plans to sell to a private collector in Bruxelles. Though they are privileged and don't

141

have to pass the security check, they believe that nothing is a safe as a good old ass. On the other hand, Sir Englishman, still floating in the pool, is unaware that he has developed malignant cancer in his ass. He inhales like a compressor from a Cuban cigar resembling very much a penis. Freud would wink at us here. Even I don't know at which state his cancer has developed, nor do I have the slightest motivation to dig in that asshole of his, but he could phone a fortune-teller woman in Romania and learn about his condition.

"Did I collide with your private space? Eh? Did I disturb your aura?" continues Rudi. If he would approach Hasan with such an attitude, the latter would finish the debate with a K.O. in 4 seconds, leaving holes in the shape of a horseshoe on the waiter's forehead and temple. But not our Britte.

"I said I was happy with your service."

"You said that the service was 'very good,' not 'excellent'! You marked 'B' on the form. Look!" says Rudolph, waving the form again. "I want to know what I am missing toward excellence! Tell me, what is good enough for Western Germans? Do you need a waiter with proper dialect to give him an 'A'?"

"I can understand what you say," confirms Britte while Nazeera monitors the valley of Jordan River with goggles, hoping that she will spot her son playing somewhere. For the sake of accuracy, German radio stations correct the news regarding the shooting in Florida. There were 15 dead, 7 seriously wounded, and 9 scratches. Firing 57 bullets, Raul Packmanchampion had 38% efficiency and was well behind Jordan's 88-89 season when he averaged 32.5 points per game on 53.8% shooting. Neither Britte nor Rudi hear it.

"And look at the last question: *Will you recommend our cafeteria to your friends?*"

"I marked 'yes,' didn't I?"

"So…tell me to whom?!?"

How come I am alone in this place, Britte is wondering. *Where is everybody?* It is almost too obvious that an innovative reader would answer: On Thursday afternoon in Stuttgart, everybody is busy assembling the Mercedes E-Class Coupe.

Rudi is forced to repeat the question. "Recommend to whom?!?"

She never met this waiter before. This dialogue runs like a 45-year-old Trabant. After careful consideration, she says, "To Klaus."

"Who's Klaus?"

"My husband. Now, would you let me go, please?" says Britte, pushing the door open.

"Your goddamn husband is not your friend; he's your relative!" corrects Rudi. "Or was he promoted into 'friend' category, recently?"

Rudolph will be fired the next day, and after two weeks, he will die near Poland in the shootout between rival gangs stealing cars in Western Europe and smuggling them to the east.

"Tell me!! Was it my accent? Was it?!?" roars Rudi after her.

Clocks hanging over Delhi InterContinental Eros's reception desk show that it is 09:07 in Mexico city, 10:07 in Jacksonville, 16:07 in Stuttgart, 17:07 in the West Bank, 19:37 in New Delhi, and 23:07 in Pyongyang. Looking for restaurants, I cross the lobby and spot Sir Englishman deeply parked in a sofa while having his shoes polished. Holding my room card in my right hand, I consider showing him the middle finger of my left hand, but being right-handed, the gesture wouldn't be genuine. I am simply not

143

able to put enough character in anything I try to do with my left hand. I eat, clean my ass, stimulate a woman's clitoris – all essential jobs – with my right hand. If the mob in Mexico City cut off my left hand one day, it wouldn't significantly diminish my surviving capabilities.

Economists possess different opinions about a beggar's contribution to his or her respective country's GDP – the controversy even more emphasized in Juanito's case, for he is too young to be included in the Mexican labor pool. A 500-pound American woman with a well-botoxed face stares at Juanito's bloody shirt wrapped around his stump. She takes her sunglasses off and replaces them with thick reading glasses, bends even lower, and continues carefully inspecting the wound for 7 minutes before declaring: "You little...little cheat!!"

I am surprised that Britte takes nothing for dinner. If she were a food taster in North Korea, she would earn even less than women sweeping highways in Sierra Leone. She will do the laundry before showering and flipping through TV channels. She will notice that there was fighting on the West Bank again, but her thumb won't stop on the news channel for more than a second, and she won't remember the number of the dead or wounded or gone mad – or the prospects of the new peace plan.

An Indian one-horned rhinoceros can speed up to 25 mph and is quite a good swimmer as well. I observe carefully the ear of the sleeping prostitute in my room. No doubt God did an excellent job with the Eustachian tube, tympanic membrane, and semicircular canals, but I admire the design of the outer ear consisting of the pinna, concha, and auditory meatus, which gather sound energy and focus it on the eardrum. I wonder how many lies of different frequencies traveled via this system to the eardrum and then to the heart of the Indian girl considered to be surplus when she was born.

Britte turns off the TV and Susan Climbingteacherassistant, 16th victim of the shooting in Jacksonville, dies in the intensive care unit. Juanito in Mexico City dies of sepsis, actually dead for three hours before collected. In the last three hours, he earned 4.5 US Dollars and 47 Pesos, not even close to Elvis, who netted 750 billion US Dollars after his death, but not a bad result for a beggar boy from poor El Arenal, Hidalgo Municipality, either. Quite promising, actually. After a couple of minutes, Israeli soldiers return a bag with Masud's body to his mother, informing her that he died of acute myelogenous leukemia during interrogation. Ms. Xhebe in Sierra Leone has been dead from the beginning of the story. Sir Englishman, sporting a new hairstyle designed by chemotherapy, will have 85% of his intestines removed; losing 70% of his mass, he will fit perfectly in the oak coffin. Raul Packmanchampion will be fastened to an electric chair after his lawyer's appeals are turned down, and I will pass away someday. Ironically, Hasan will never die, in a way. After his physical death, a newly arrived illegal immigrant will take his passport and his vegetable kiosk and continue living happily using Hasan's identity. Britte will die in Germany, and Klaus will, as well. If not, Lufthansa will transport his body from wherever for a fee, which can't be disclosed at the moment. It is also not clear yet whether he would earn a discount on account of his miles and more mileage.

Rotterdam Zoo announced that a white rhino calf was born in the afternoon. Zookeepers artificially inseminated his mother, Teresa, 16 months ago. A healthy calf, named Rosenthal, weights 86 kg and is the first of its species to be born in captivity.

The Visitors

Jenny Palmer

There were two of them who came the last time. My house is just about the right size for one visitor. When there are two, it is a bit of a tight squeeze. Trips to the bathroom are difficult. Timing is all important. I usually give up my bedroom and sleep in the spare room, which is full of books and doubles up as a study. There are so many ideas floating around in there, that I find it difficult to switch off. In the mornings, I will often feel shattered but still feel duty bound to ask the visitors how they have slept. I already know the answer. They have got the best room in the house.

I first started doing Airbnb for a bit of extra cash. Then I found I liked the company. You can get lonely living out here, with only the sheep to talk to and the birds. I don't usually get involved with the guests. I prefer to leave them to their own devices. This time I told them to be sure and bring their walking shoes. I live right out in the sticks, five miles to the nearest town and the bus service is poor. If they want to go anywhere they must walk. I prefer it if the visitors go out during the day. But the weather was against them. It rained all week and the ground was too muddy to walk on.

It would have been a struggle for them to get any shopping. There was no way they could have carried it home. The bus stop is at least half an hour away on foot. So, they came with me when I went shopping. In the end, we decided to cook together. I enjoy trying out new recipes, anyway. They were fond of using superfoods like quinoa and blueberries. It made a change from my normal diet.

They said they wanted to know what it was like living in the countryside from first-hand experience. Where they came from, it was overcrowded. You couldn't move without bumping into people. They were looking for a place to move with more space. One day, when we were out, I suggested we visit the local museum. It has been done recently up with lottery money. It has gone all touchy-feely and there are recordings of bird calls and people talking in local accents. But there are some good displays and, if you follow it through, you can trace the history of mankind from prehistoric times right to the present. They made notes all the way through.

Another day I took them to a textile museum, where they could see the actual cotton weaving machines working, clattering away just like in the old days. That really knocked them out. They said they had never seen anything like it and took video footage to show back home. On the strength of that, I took them to the nearby abbey, where Cistercian monks had once laboured, cultivating crops, rearing sheep, re-routing the water courses to take away their sewage. The visitors were impressed by the self-sufficiency of the monks in previous centuries.

"You never know," they commented. "It may come to that one day."

The highlight of their stay was our trip to the Yorkshire Dales. We visited Gordale Scar with its gigantic stone structures and on the hills above Malham we spotted evidence of Neolithic life in the form of stone cairns. I told them that ancient man had once lived alongside woolly mammoths and used their tusks to fashion into tools. They were curious and wanted to know why these ancient people had preferred to live up on the rock terraces rather than down in the valley.

"It must have been warmer on the hills," I said, guessing. "I expect it was to avoid the retreating ice flows."

"You mean the climate was different then?" they asked.

I was surprised they hadn't realised that.

148

Their visit coincided with the American elections. They joined me in watching some of the coverage on television. It was the usual story. The two rival candidates were slogging it out, taking chunks out of each other.

"The stakes are high," I explained. "They are fighting over who will be the next leader of the free world."

"Why do they call it free?" One of them asked. "Where we come from, we decide our leaders by consensus."

"I suppose it is just human nature to want to be top dog," I said.

"Hasn't that sort of behaviour been consigned to the animal kingdom yet?"

"Unfortunately, not," I said. I found I was getting defensive, although there really was nothing to defend. It was despicable behaviour.

"If this new man wins, he says he will reverse all previous policies. Won't he be setting the planet back? Is that wise? Won't it lead to more global warming and the inevitable extinction of life on the planet?"

"Well, yes, if you put it that way," I said. "I suppose it will."

"And is he to be trusted with the nuclear codes? What exactly is his appeal?"

I wondered where they had been for the past year and a half. After all, it was all anyone had been talking about. I said that his appeal lay with people who felt left behind, people who had worked in coal mining and steel production in what they called the rustbelt. Their jobs had disappeared due to global capitalism when those industries had moved to other countries where the labour was cheaper. The previous government hadn't been paying enough attention to them so now they wanted to change the government.

They looked disconcerted, as if they were hearing it for the first time.

149

"But it's a global phenomenon," I said, "this shift to the right. We had it here with Brexit."

They just stared at me. They didn't seem to know what I was talking about. I wondered where they had been all their lives.

"But can't people see that nations need to work together to forge common policies,' they said, 'that it's their only hope, if they are not to destroy their planet."

They were clearly getting agitated. I don't know why I hadn't noticed it before but when I looked at them, their eyes had a glazed, transparent quality. They seemed otherworldly, somehow. I put it down to tiredness. It was time for bed.

"Our work is done here," they said, as they left the next day.

I couldn't understand why they had gone so quickly. Then a letter came and everything fell into place. They thanked me for my hospitality. They explained they were from a planet in a far-away galaxy. Their planet had used up its resources and was fast becoming uninhabitable. They had been sent out on an exploratory mission to look into the possibility of re-settling elsewhere. Earth had appealed to them at first but when faced with the reality that I had made them aware of, they had changed their minds. They were sorry. I imagined them hot-footing it to some other planet and waited with trepidation for my next visitors to come.

Index of Authors

Other Publications by Bridge House

Tales from the Upper Room

edited by Janice Gilbert, Debz Hobbs-Wyatt and Gini Scanlan

Poems and Short Stories by the Canvey Writers, St Nicholas Group, who meet in the upstairs room…

You will be wowed by the dark tales: a modern day Little Red Riding Hood – as you have never seen her before. You will wait for the Reaper to come and you'll encounter ghosts in different forms. You will laugh at how Mavis and cat, Cuddles, and a glass of Lambrusco manage to start World War III, and how a job search lands aging Mr Montegoo the perfect job. You will read about war, about hate, and about love. You will encounter the power of what-if moments, love that endures, lovers that got away and the effect of the choices we make in life.

Proceeds from the sale of this book will be donated to Havens Hospices

Order from Amazon:

Paperback: ISBN 978-1-907335-19-8

Extraordinary

by Dawn Knox

From the furthest reaches of the universe, to the inside of a cardboard box, assorted characters play deadly games with their victims while others play practical jokes on angels or dirty tricks on aliens. Some have good intentions, others are scoundrels and a few are truly evil – but all of them are EXTRAORDINARY.

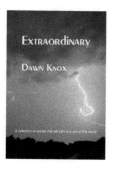

"A wonderful collection of amazing stories. An enjoyable read." (*Amazon*)

Order from Amazon:

Paperback: ISBN 978-1-907335-51-8
eBook: ISBN 978-1-907335-52-5

Baubles

edited by Debz Hobbs-Wyatt and Gill James

The challenge was to write a bauble of a story. So we have a
varied selection of snippets that sparkle. Once again we feel
privileged to publish this fine group of writers. Each story is
different and glitters in its own way.

"A great range of stories and styles here. A story for everyone.
Talented, contemporary writers writing about issues that
engage you." (*Amazon*)

Order from Amazon:

Paperback: ISBN 978-1-907335-46-4
eBook: ISBN 978-1-907335-47-1